One and
Three Quarters

SHRIKANT
BOJEWAR

One and Three Quarters

TRANSLATED BY
VIKRANT PANDE

eka

First published in Marathi as *Pavane Don Payancha Manus* in 2007 by Deshmukh & Co Publishers Pvt. Ltd

Published in English as *One and Three Quarters* in 2024 by Eka, an imprint of Westland Books, a division of Nasadiya Technologies Private Limited

No. 269/2B, First Floor, 'Irai Arul', Vimalraj Street, Nethaji Nagar, Alapakkam Main Road, Maduravoyal, Chennai 600095

Westland, the Westland logo, Eka and the Eka logo are the trademarks of Nasadiya Technologies Private Limited, or its affiliates.

ISBN: 9789360458249

10 9 8 7 6 5 4 3 2 1

Typeset by Jojy Philip, New Delhi

Printed at Nutech Print Services, India

Chapter 1

While the schoolchildren rushed out of the school building making a racket, Langdya Pitambar continued sitting in the classroom. The class teacher had handed over the marksheets for the mid-term examination. There were quite a few zeroes there. In a way this was convenient as Langdya could easily add the digit 2 or 3 before the zero! That way he could buy a day before the truth was revealed. For he was sure that his father and Gengane-master would meet at the local liquor shack and the topic of Langdya's marksheet would certainly come up. No doubt it would lead to a fracas between the two. Langdya could visualise the scene vividly.

The local hooch distillery was behind Naru Pingtya's house. Gengane-master came at night, removed his slippers outside, and entered. Naru shouted that very moment, '*Arre* master, how dare you? Pay your dues first! Else you are not welcome here.' Gengane-master was desperate for a drink. He carried his bent body to the counter where Naru sat and pleaded, '*Arre* Naru, I will pay! My school is *vina anudaanit*, a non-subsidised one. The moment I get the grant, I will clear all the dues.' Naru got up from the counter. There were seven others drinking in his shop. He commanded all of them to stand and they all did—mutely. They were drunk and as they stood, they swayed a little, trying to balance themselves. No one knew why Naru had ordered them to stand, but none of them had the courage to challenge their 'hooch provider'.

Naru stared at them the way a local police inspector glares at suspects lined up for enquiry. He asked the first man in the row, 'Hey Shirpat, what is your qualification?'

Shirpat shivered at the question. 'Are you now going to demand a matriculation certificate before you serve us liquor? Baba, I am matric fail. And don't ask me to tell the name of my school. It still sends shivers down my spine.'

Naru put a gentle hand on Shirpat's shoulder and said, '*Arre*, it is quite credible that you reached the level of the matriculate exam. If you are so learned, why don't you tell me what "non-subsidised" means.'

'What? I don't know what you are saying. Don't ask what such difficult words mean. Tchah! What a put-downer!' Shirpat gulped down the drink from his tumbler in one go and then rubbed a piece of pickle on his tongue. By then Gengane-master had found a place to sit on the wooden bench. Naru said, addressing him, 'I am serving you for free today, but you must explain what non-subsidised means.'

Gengane-master was quite overwhelmed when he saw Naru's yearning to learn something new. He concluded that if there was such love and fascination for the Marathi language in rural Maharashtra, the angst which the urban elite were showing with regard to the fear of the language losing its importance seemed quite misplaced. Naru dragged a stool near Gengane-master and sat on it. Chiptya, Naru's help, too wiped his hands on his dirty shirt and waited expectantly for the master-saheb to explain. Gengane-master was taking his time. He downed half the tumbler in one go and then picked up a piece of pickle to suck on.

Naru held his hand and said beseechingly, 'Master, please tell me before you empty the tumbler. I have been hearing about this non-subsidised business for a while now. Not one fucker can explain what it means.'

Before Gengane-master could speak, Shirpat shouted, 'Naru, we are tired of standing. Please, can we sit now?'

Naru turned to see all of them still standing obediently. He snapped at Chiptya, 'Fucker, are you going to keep your customers standing? The customer is God! Our kitchens are stocked thanks to them. They are drunks, I can understand, but why are *you* behaving like one?' Chiptya stood up and gently helped Shirpat to sit down. Seeing him, others followed suit and they all settled down. Now it was Chiptya's turn to ask Gengane-master, 'Master-saheb, tell us about this non-subsidised thing.' Gengane-master was about to take a sip when he saw Langdya Pitambar's father entering the shack. His name was Ajabrao but he was known all over the village as Langdya's father. Seeing Gengane-master already there, Ajabrao approached him. He said, addressing Naru, 'Today, Master's drinks are on me! After all, the way he has taught Pitambar, he deserves a treat!' Gengane-master put forth his pickle-stained hand for a 'hi-fi'.

Chiptya put a tumbler of local hooch near Ajabrao and pushed the bowl of pickle towards him. Naru warned Ajabrao, 'Ajabya, don't open your mouth now. Today master-saheb is going to tell us what non-subsidised means.'

Gengane-master downed his tumbler and said, 'I will not tell lies.'

Naru banged his fist on the table and growled, 'I will thrash you if you dare!' Gengane ignored Naru's theatrics. The comment was meant for Langdya's father. Gengane continued, 'I am a teacher by profession and I shall not tell lies just because you are treating me to free liquor. Langdya must have tampered with his marksheet. He has got zero in almost all subjects.'

Ajabrao's anger knew no bounds. He stood up, clutched Gengane's collar, and shouted, 'Bloody master! Is the government paying you to twiddle your thumbs? If my son fails this year in the final exam, I will cut you in half and stuff you like a pickle. I will go and thrash that son of a bitch now. The bugger's making a *chootiya* out of his father. How dare he!'

Naru was disappointed. He said, '*Abey* Ajabya, is that anything new? Langdya failing in class? We were about to hear Master-saheb talk about non-subsidised education, and you burst into your own song!'

Langdya's father sat quietly and gulped down two more tumblers of liquor. He then got up, kicking Gengane-master's chair. He shouted, 'You sit here and spout wisdom before Naru. But let your children in school fail, you bastard. I will go home and break the other leg of that cripple.' Kicking open the door of the shack, Ajabrao stepped out.

⁂

The sound of the door being kicked brought Langdya Pitambar back to his senses. His reverie broke. The marksheet in his hand fluttered in the wind as the door of his classroom banged shut. He had seen, with his mental 'fast forward', what he feared would happen in the liquor shack that evening. However, positive thoughts overtook him and, hoping that things wouldn't pan out exactly the way he had visualised them, he took out his pen and added a few numbers before the zeroes. He totalled the new marks and, folding the marksheet into his geography book, stepped out of the classroom. As he stepped on the main road, a black cat jumped from a wall and crossed the road. Before Langdya could react, she jumped onto the other wall and disappeared. Langdya was incensed. 'Damn it, you cat! Now the scene is going to be repeated tonight just the way I dreamt! Fuck you!'

The cat heard Langdya's curses as she wiped her whiskers, but chose to ignore him. She muttered to herself, 'I had to scram as that Deshmukh's dog Tipya was after me. What can I do if Langdya was crossing the street that very minute? He doesn't study, he tells lies, and then he blames me and calls me a motherfucker!'

She climbed the wall to glance at the street. Langdya was on his way home. As one of his legs was a few inches shorter than the other, he walked with a pronounced limp that made the bag on his back bob up and down with each step. Ensuring that Tipya was nowhere in sight, she jumped down the wall and walked towards the Pawar household. This was the time Mrs Pawar cleared the plates after lunch. Today being Friday, she was quite certain that she would find a piece of mutton or two. The thought of a juicy mutton piece ran a shiver through her body as she spread her claws.

Pitambar limped his way home. He had never enjoyed school. All his classmates were now in the tenth while he was stuck in the seventh grade. Except for the Physical Training (PT) class, he never enjoyed any other subject. His father had hoped that Gengane-teacher's tuition would help him clear the exams. But what could Gengane do? Langdya's mind was like a dried-up well. Any amount of effort to send a bucket down would not yield water. And Gengane's teaching was like trying to fill that well with spoonfuls of water. On top of it, Gengane's pet cat would somehow irk Langdya. On the very first day of class, Gengane had asked Langdya to write an essay titled 'My Ambition'. After seeing the topic, Langdya sat there chewing his pen cap. Then he wrote the first line: 'India is essentially an agricultural country.'

Gengane-master sat nearly eight feet away. The cat was near Langdya's feet. After Langdya wrote the first line, she stood up and went near Gengane to lick his toe. Gengane shouted, 'You fucker, where does "agriculture" figure when the essay is about one's ambition?' Langdya was taken aback. How the hell was Gengane able to see what he had written, sitting so far away? He stared at the cat with suspicion and disbelief. The cat sat near the wall, her eyes shut, blissfully ignoring Langdya. Langdya threw his notebook at her but missed. Their enmity, which began that day, continued to grow since then.

Gengane was trying his best to impart an education worth the tuition fee he was charging, but all his efforts were in vain, for Langdya couldn't understand a word of what the teacher taught. Langdya told himself each day that reading and writing were not his forte. He somehow spent his time in the hope that his father would say to him one day, 'Quit school and take up a job somewhere.'

A thought crossed his mind: 'That Bhadya fucker would have told his dad that the mid-term marksheet has been issued today.' He muttered a few juicy epithets for Bhadya. 'That Bhadya is an intelligent guy and gets good marks. That's fine. Let him roll up the marksheet and stick it up whosoever's ass he wishes to. Why the hell does he try to meddle with others' lives?' Langdya muttered as he limped his way home, his bag swinging on his back with each step. He recalled the black cat having crossed his path when he left school and once again wondered whether he should show the marksheet to his father. He was sure his father would ask for it and he was doubly sure that Gengane would talk about it in the evening at the liquor vend. What should he do? Langdya's mind, sharp in subjects other than those taught at school, whirled with rapid speed. He began spinning stories to tell at home.

I won't go home now. I will while away some time at the bus stand, look at the cinema posters at the talkies. Stand near the paanwallah for a while and collect a few half-burnt cigarette stubs … The idea was to reach home as late as possible. The scene at home when he walked in would be as follows.

'Is this the time to come home? When did your school get over? And were you eating cowdung all this while.'

'No, not eating. I was watching it.'

'Better tell me the truth, okay? And if you dare lie, I will whack you with the tyre-tube. Believe me!'

'We were given the mid-term marksheet today.'

'I know that. Why do you think I am here to welcome you home?'

'I was walking home reading the marksheet when I saw Bapurao's buffalo approaching me.'

'Forget the buffalo. Tell me where your marksheet is.'

'That is what I was telling you. That buffalo grabbed the marksheet from my hands and gobbled it up.'

Langdya's father kept staring at his son wide-mouthed for a while. Realising that his jaws were aching, he got back to his senses and said, 'You mean the buffalo ate your marksheet? Why? Maybe you told her that she will give more milk after eating your marksheet. Or perhaps someone told her that eating a seventh-standard marksheet leads to a quicker pregnancy!'

'I don't know about that. She ate it up—that's what matters!'

'What the hell were you doing for five hours then? Or were you pleading with the buffalo to regurgitate your marksheet?'

'Yes.'

'Yes? Really, you motherfucker!'

'I was following her. I was hoping I would find the marksheet in her dung. But she never shat!'

Ajabrao kept looking at his son in disbelief. Then, as if resigned to his fate, he finally asked, 'Well, did you pass or not?'

'Yes. I did.'

'It is quite a coincidence that Bapurao's buffalo had to find your marksheet, of all things, to eat. Now I can imagine Bapurao milking her tomorrow morning to find History, Geography, Arithmetic and English coming out of her teats!' Ajabrao laughed loudly at his own joke.

Langdya snapped out of his reverie when he heard his father's laughter in his mind. He wondered if the story of the buffalo eating the marksheet would fly. Just then, he noticed a cat coming out of Karjatmal Marwari's shop. '*Arre*, this is Gengane-master's cat. What is she doing here?' Langdya wondered. The cat stopped for a moment and looked at Langdya. She gave him a knowing smile but Langdya didn't smile back. Instead, he picked up a stone to fling at her lest she cross his path once more. The cat dodged the stone easily and cursed at him, 'Lazy bugger! He doesn't study, keeps a roving eye on Gengane's wife, and when he fails, he takes his frustration out on me. Now I will deliberately cross the street.'

Muttering, the cat crossed the lane. Langdya was frustrated. A cat had crossed his path twice since he left school. He was convinced that his stories wouldn't work and he had no option but to show the marksheet to his father.

He was hungry. He remembered his mother was roasting big brinjals to make baingan bharta in the morning. The very thought of hot bhakris made him drool. Forget the marksheet and its consequences! I will hand over the forged marksheet to Bappa. Once Gengane tells him the truth, I will figure out a way to face him. Now all he could think of was baingan bharta and bhakri. 'Fuck Gengane and the marksheet!' He cursed under his breath and started walking rapidly towards his house. The bag on his back swung faster with each step. Gengane's cat, roaming near Chandu Sheth's shop, saw Langdya walk home with a determined step and muttered, 'Even Gengane's wife is eyeing this fellow. Gengane is an idiot not to see all this!'

Langdya reached home and hung his bag on a wooden peg on the wall. He perfunctorily poured water on his legs and arms from a bucket kept near the entrance. He was hungry and didn't bother to clean his limbs well. He shouted, 'Ma, I am hungry! Lay out the plates.'

His mother put a spoonful of baingan bharta on a plate and took a bajra bhakri from near the stove. Langdya took a few chillies hanging from a rope in the kitchen. He had barely started chewing a mouthful when he heard his father's rasping cough. After taking the first long puff of his beedi, Ajabrao would, for the next five minutes, hold his chest while cough racked his body. But that had not deterred him from his habit. Ajabrao entered the house. The moment he spotted Langdya's bag hanging from the wooden peg, he shouted, 'Shevanta, don't serve food to that bastard. Let that motherfucker die hungry.'

Langdya quickly began gulping down his food. It was likely that Gengane-master and his father had met. It was evident that his father had heard from Gengane about his exemplary performance in the test!

Shevanta quickly served another bhakri to Langdya, saying, 'What did the master tell your father? Have you failed the test or what?' Langdya stuffed another mouthful before answering, 'What can I do if that Gengane fellow doesn't know how to teach properly? I attend his tuition regularly and also solve the maths problems diligently. Still he fails me!'

While the mother-son duo continued their chat, Langdya's father entered the kitchen fuming with anger. 'Show me your marksheet.' Langdya's stomach was now full and helping the wheels of his mind to turn faster than normal. He decided not to show the marksheet to his father. The buffalo story seemed plausible now on a full stomach, and he decided to stick to it.

'Bapurao's buffalo gobbled up my marksheet.'

Ajabrao was taken aback. He had not expected such an unusual response.

'What? Are you delirious? What nonsense are you blabbering?'

'I am telling the truth. I stepped out of the school holding my marksheet and there she was, Bapurao's buffalo, standing on the road. She grabbed my marksheet and started chewing on it.' Langdya had barely narrated his story when a fat tomcat created a clamour as he jumped from the kitchen loft chasing a rat. He missed his aim and struck Langdya's bag, which was hanging by the hook, instead. Both the tomcat and Langdya's bag fell on the floor. The contents of the bag spilled out. And there lay the Geography book, wide open— the same book in which Langdya had hidden his marksheet. It now lay near his father's feet.

Not only had the tomcat lost its quarry but also suffered the humiliation of falling like a stone in the presence of all the residents. He stood in a corner wiping his paws when he spotted the embers of anger in Langdya's eyes. He muttered to himself, 'This fellow is shooting daggers at me. Did I deliberately jump on his bag? It seems some paper fell out of the book. I wonder if it is a love letter written by Gengane-master's wife. I recall Ghaari, the one with the beautiful grey eyes, telling me the other day that this Langdya and Master's wife make eyes at each other whenever Master is busy elsewhere. Anyway, why should I care? Let the husband do whatever he has to.' The tomcat ran out of the house, mumbling.

By then Ajabrao had started examining the marksheet. The marks, changed by Langdya, were screaming for attention. He pulled his son affectionately towards him and said, 'You have passed, Langdya! Why did you lie that the buffalo ate your marksheet?'

'I thought you wouldn't believe me, so I was hesitant,' Langdya said as he sat down to finish dinner. Shevanta put another bhakri in his plate. She couldn't believe whatever Langdya had said.

Stoking the fire in the stove, she asked, 'Did you really pass?'

Langdya answered, 'What do you think? Did I change the marks on my own?'

Shevanta could gauge that Langdya, while trying to be rhetorical, had actually blurted out the truth. The lips may lie but the heart knew what the truth was. On the other hand, Ajabrao was thrilled to see the marks. He was making plans to go to Naru's hooch shack and down two glasses of liquor. The 'fast forward scene' of his father going to Naru's where he would surely meet Gengane-master appeared before Langdya's eyes. The wheels of his mind were now working rapidly. He had to find a way out!

✍

Langdya stepped out of the house. In fact, he used to wait every day for Gengane-master to leave his house and walk to the bar. Every evening Langdya used to go to Gengane-master's house for tuition. It was an hour-long lesson, but Langdya's attention would be divided between looking at the cat and eyeing Gengane's wife. Gengane's cat Ghaari used to keep a vigil on Langdya, as if she had been asked to do so. In the evening, while Langdya was being tutored by Gengane, his wife would be dusting around the house and lighting the lamps in the pooja room and in front of the tulsi shrub in the courtyard. Langdya could see the tulsi shrub from where he sat. As Gengane's wife would bend to light the lamp near the shrub in the receding light and increasing darkness of the evening, Langdya would get to see her ample bosom. He would often wonder: 'Does she not wear anything under her blouse?' It would be impossible for Langdya, after such a tantalising view, to focus on either Maths or Geography. Gengane's cat would try her best to distract Langdya as he was ogling Gengane's wife and her bosom. She would often climb the cement platform around the tulsi shrub to prevent Langdya from getting a clear view. But the small cat was not enough to block the ample bosom. While the cat tried her best, Langdya would be happy to capture the image in an instant. At times the cat would deliberately push the lamp away with her paws. That was enough to spoil the moment while Gengane's wife picked up the lamp. But of late Ghaari had stopped trying to distract Langdya's attention. She had recounted the episode many times, adding her own spice to it, to all her other cat friends, including the tomcats.

In the night, while the town slept, the cats and tomcats from around the village would assemble below the light pole near Shinde's garage. They gossiped about the events of the day until it was time to return to their respective alleys by midnight. The rats would come out after midnight in search of food. Till then the cats would spend time chatting and socialising. One day the event at Gengane-master's house was the topic of their evening gossip.

All the tomcats, cats and kittens had assembled. Some of the tomcats lay stretched out, relaxing. The cats were busy chatting, all at the same time. The black cat from Nago Patil's house said, 'That Patil doesn't care if it is day or night. Poor Mrs Patil gets crushed like a flower.'

To this, another cat said, 'If you are so sympathetic to her, why don't you scratch Patil's dick. Till his wound heals, Patil ma'am can breathe easy.'

Four of the cats assembled there extended their paws for a 'hi-fi'. Then, Ghaari from Gengane's house caught their attention. 'Today something extraordinary happened in our house.' All the tomcats perked their ears to listen attentively. Their interest lay in her and not Gengane-master. She cleared her throat and began, 'I have often mentioned how Langdya, who comes for tuition, ogles Gengane's wife all the time. Gengane-master gives me a roti dipped in milk. So, naturally I am loyal to him and keep an eye on Langdya. Today Langdya was thirsty while the tuition was on and he asked Master for a tumbler of water. Gengane-master said, "Go to the kitchen and take water from the mud pot kept there." When Langdya went into the kitchen I followed him. While Langdya was having water, Gengane-master's wife came in. She let her saree pallu fall and then pulled Langdya's face into her bosom. Langdya coughed loudly and then came out into the room, his face flushed.'

One of the tomcats commented, 'The flames of lust … is that why it is called kitchen?'

'Don't make stupid comments,' Ghaari reprimanded him.

Another cat said, 'Tell me, Ghaari, is your master impotent?'

Ghaari was irritated at the question and replied, 'Tchah! He is a good man.'

The topic ended there but, from that day onwards, Ghaari stopped trying to prevent Langdya from enjoying his peek at Gengane-master's wife's bosom. The wife continued to show her cleavage whenever she got a chance. Now she even began to leave some buttons on her blouse open to allow for more flesh to be visible.

After the tuition Langdya would come home for a hearty meal. Gengane-master would leave for his daily ritual at Naru's country bar, while Langdya would finish his meal, quickly wash his hands, and head for Master's house. Until now, he had not dared to enter Gengane-master's house in his absence. He would while away time roaming around. Today too he had started walking towards Master's house, but he was preoccupied. He had to find a way to prevent Master from going to Naru's bar. His mind was working at full speed when he spotted the music teacher, Alaknanda Deshpande walking briskly towards the four-hundred-year-old mud fort in the village. Something clicked in Langdya's mind and he decided to follow her instead of going towards Gengane-master's house.

Gengane-master stepped out of the house and spotted Langdya. Langdya didn't try to hide himself. He said, approaching Gengane, 'Master, I saw Mrs Deshpande going towards the mud fort. She seemed to be in a hurry.'

'So?'

'Habib-sir was following her at a brisk pace,' Langdya added.

'You fucker, why are you poking your nose into matters that have nothing to do with you? Go home and study,' barked Gengane before leaving. Langdya waited in the shadows, watching the master. Gengane-master walked a few yards and then, turning around to see if there was anyone in sight, proceeded quickly towards the mud fort. Langdya clapped in glee. Ghaari was watching Langdya, but she was unable to understand why he was so excited. For Langdya had not even bothered to glance at Gengane's house. Confused by Langdya's behaviour, she decided to follow her master. She was worried that he might be in trouble. But while following the master, she had to cross Langdya's path, irritating him to no end. 'That motherfucker of a cat! Why does she have to cross my path?' Langdya's mission was yet to be completed, and the fact that the cat had crossed his path made him worry if it would reach its logical end.

Hobbling on his handicapped legs, Langdya approached Ismail Garage. It belonged to Habib-sir's brother. A few cars would be permanently parked outside this garage. In fact, Langdya had seen a car parked there for the past five years. He had never seen anyone drive it. There were two things that he had never seen move: one was the car and the other was the blind beggar woman who sat below the staircase of Dr Pawar's clinic. He used to wonder if the car had ever been on the road, if it had ever moved. Likewise, he wondered if the old blind beggar ever moved to take a piss or a dump.

Langdya spotted Ismail under the car, half his body, from below the waist, jutting out. He was working in the light of a naked bulb connected to red and yellow wires on the ground. His assistant was placing tools on Ismail's extended hand as and when he needed them. Instructions like 'Munna, pass me number 3,' or 'Munna, the grease box,' could be heard. Langdya often passed the time watching them at work. He often dreamt of buying a car one day. He imagined that the car would have some trouble and he would take it to Ismail's garage. Ismail would be under the car shouting, 'Munna, pass me number 2 please.' He had dreamt of all that. But today he didn't have time for day dreaming. He was looking for Habib-sir. After dinner, Habib-sir had a habit of coming there and enjoying a paan at the Shevade Tambu Gruha—Shevade Paan House—sitting on a stool. As expected, Langdya spotted Habib-sir there. He approached him saying, 'Sir.'

Habib-sir's mouth was full of betel juice. He was in no mood to spit that out to speak to Langdya. He pursed his lips, somehow managing to retain all the juice in his mouth. 'What is it, Langdya?'

Langdya came closer. 'Sir, that Deshpande-madam! She went towards the mud fort just now.'

Habib-sir didn't show much interest in Langdya's information. He said in a casual tone, 'So?'

'Gengane-master followed her there.'

The moment Habib-sir heard that, he jumped down from the high stool. Making a spout around his lips with two fingers, he let loose a stream of betel juice on to the ground and said, 'Is that so?'

'Yes,' answered Langdya and excused himself. Habib-sir put on his sandals and walked briskly towards the mud fort. He said, shouting to Ismail, 'I will be back in a while.' Ismail merely grunted in acknowledgement from below the car.

Langdya mused, 'Well, things are moving as expected. I hope Ghaari's crossing my path doesn't create any hurdle.' Recalling the cat made him recall Gengane's wife, but he didn't want to risk going in that direction. He now felt reassured that even if his father went to Naru's bar, he wouldn't meet Gengane that evening. At least the secret of his marksheet would remain a secret for another day. With this assurance, his limp reduced considerably. He whistled gayly as he walked home.

At that moment, a fat tomcat walked out of Shankar's flour mill. He said to another tomcat, 'Why are you sharpening your nails on that iron pole? Find some table or a chair.'

The other tomcat replied, 'Just for a change.'

The fat one spotted Langdya and said, 'There goes Langdya. Remember Ghaari telling us how Gengane-master's wife hugged him.'

The other tomcat looked at Langdya and said, 'That brat looks like a smart alec. But Ghaari tells me he gets pretty upset if a cat crosses his path. Come, let's cross his path and watch the fun!'

'Come on,' the other one nodded. The tomcats crossed Langdya's path one after another, making him fume in anger. 'First that Ghaari, and now these two! Is my plan going to flop?' Langdya shivered at the thought. His mind started churning furiously. Why did Deshpande-madam walk so briskly in the evening towards the mud fort?

Something seemed to be brewing between Gengane-master and Deshpande-madam. Mr Kavthekar was the earlier music teacher. The music teacher had three main tasks. The first one was to play the harmonium while the children sang an invocation to Goddess Saraswati and the national anthem at 11 a.m. The second task was to sing the song '*Jhanda ooncha rahe hamara*' on 26 January, and the third and final task was to sing the same song on 15 August. Kavthekar reminded one of a doll with frizzled hair stuck on a pole. He would teach music to students of the 5th and 6th standards. There was a music period for the 8th and 10th standards as well, but he would rarely get a chance to take those classes, for the school's headmaster, Dhamale, would call him to his room the moment the national anthem was over. The headmaster's attendant, a man with a torn earlobe, would stand near Kavthekar and, with a slight nod and raising his eyebrows, indicate that he was to meet the headmaster in his office. Kavthekar would rush to meet the headmaster and ask, as soon as he entered his room, 'Sir, did you call for me?'

'Yes, Kavthekar. Govindvar-sir is behind schedule, so I suggest you give your 10 B music class slot to him. In any case, the best the students can do after learning music is to become beggars!' The last line would pierce poor Kavthekar's heart but he would keep mum. It was probably such comments that had made him a little weird. For example, he had taken four or five of the worst singers from Class 6 and would make them practise extensively. Listening to their out-of-tune and hoarse singing, the headmaster would comment, 'Kavthekar-sir, why don't you pick children with slightly sweet voices. Listening to these kids is sheer torture!'

Kavthekar would reply, 'Sir, it is easy for anyone with a good voice to sound melodious. The challenge is to make these hoarse voices sing in tune.' Kavthekar, it seems, had mastered the art of finding the worst of the singers.

Kavthekar's wife was a timid soul. She and Kavthekar were poles apart. He had a dull, boring personality while she was quite attractive. But she was a simple woman. Kavthekar would never allow her to step out of the house. One day while Kavthekar was in school, a few relatives came home. They were distant cousins of Kavthekar's. They said they would only have a cup of tea and leave, but Kavthekar's wife wanted to give them a return gift, a blouse-piece at least. But there was no money at home. Mrs Kavthekar stepped out of the house and got a blouse-piece from Fullubhai's shop on credit. She saved the day.

But, fifteen days later, she was seen going away on Fullubhai's motorcycle never to return. Kavthekar was devastated. Soon, he lost his mind. These days, he was seen hovering near Fullubhai's shop with a harmonium hung around his neck. Whenever a young woman stepped out of the shop, he accosted her and started playing the harmonium saying, 'Come on now, sing the national anthem, sing *"Jana gana mana adhinayak jaya he"'*, till Fullubhai's servant shooed him away.

Well, what was the school to do when the music teacher had lost his marbles? As such the school was one with no grant. Gengane-master, who didn't know the difference between an accordion and a harmonium, was asked by Headmaster Dhamale to take charge during the singing of the national anthem. In this school with a no-grant status, Gengane's salary, which was three thousand on paper but fifteen hundred in hand, increased by another three hundred.

When Gengane picked up the harmonium, the headmaster instructed, 'First the invocation to Goddess Saraswati and then the national song.'

Gengane got flustered. 'I don't know how to play the national song. Why not play the national anthem instead?'

Dhamale would have thrown Gengane out, but he was a kind-hearted man. And the fact that Gengane was a good Maths teacher came to his rescue. Dhamale probably thought that it was okay for a Maths teacher to not know the national song. The unexpected raise of three hundred rupees was something Gengane enjoyed for less than a year. One morning Alaknanda Deshpande came to meet Dhamale-sir with a letter from a very senior board member, and the very next day, she was appointed as the music teacher. Gengane's salary was reduced by three hundred rupees. Naru's income too reduced by the same amount. Though Gengane did not skip having a glass of the local arrack every night, he often drank on credit. Whenever Naru brought up his dues, Gegane would start talking about how the school was likely to receive a grant soon, and how everyone's salaries would go up.

Well, the whole purpose of this flashback was to tell you that Gengane dreamt of a day when Alaknanda-madam would get caught in some scandal or the other and be relieved from her job, thus giving him a chance to earn back the extra three hundred rupees.

There was an ancient mud fort from Shivaji's times. It was a mini fortress of sorts, but quite small. The fortress lay in darkness, with shrubs and trees all around. Quite naturally, the men and women who were seen entering and leaving the area under the cover of darkness were not in the category of 'gentlemen' or 'ladies'. Gengane was curious to know why Alaknanda Deshpande was walking towards the fortress so late in the evening. He walked in the hope that he would uncover some scandal, the result of which would be her dismissal and a consequent bump in his salary. It was a tempting thought. He walked around the fortress, scanning the bushes and trees in the deepening darkness.

⧜

Habib-sir taught Hindi at school. It was all right for other teachers to be addressed simply as 'master' or 'sir', but Habib-sir was strictly 'Habib-sir.' He loved to teach. He was a partner in his brother's garage and thus enjoyed a double income. He could be seen wearing a terylene shirt, a pair of expensive trousers, and he always had a fragrant paan in his mouth. His brother would often drop him off to school in his car. He thus walked with an air of importance. 'He cannot teach Hindi as his mother tongue is Urdu,' was the common refrain, expressed in hushed voices.

One day Gengane reached school after visiting Naru's country bar. At the school gate he saw Habib-sir getting down from the car. Gengane smiled and said, spitting on the ground, 'The Hindi teacher does not know Hindi but comes to school in a car. The Maths teacher knows Mathematics but doesn't have even a tyre, let alone a cycle.'

Habib-sir acted as if he had not heard Gengane's comment, but since then, he nursed a grudge against Gengane. This was something Langdya was aware of. His interests lay in such gossip rather than in studies. And so, today Langdya was going to use this knowledge to his advantage. Habib-sir walked towards the fort, hopeful that he would stumble across a scandal involving Gengane-master and Deshpande-madam. His obese body was not meant for such vigorous activities; as a result, he huffed and puffed as he walked. It was as if some strange force was propelling him towards his destination.

⌘

Langdya was in two minds—not two minds, but three, so to speak! He was keen to go home and stretch out on his bed, but he was also keen to know what his father was blabbering at Naru's liquor den. And at the same time, he was desperately eager to see whatever was happening at the mud fort. Deshpande-madam didn't seem to be the kind of person who would have an affair on the sly—at least she didn't show any such signs in school. He could go and find out for himself, but if Habib-sir and Gengane-master spotted him there, it would be embarrassing. Besides, two tomcats had crossed his path that evening. He could have ignored one tomcat, but two of them crossing his path was a tad too much.

The two tomcats stood at the corner of a road near a tea stall, watching Langdya. Seeing them, Langdya picked up a stone with his toes and, taking it in his hand, flung it in the direction of one of the tomcats. 'You fuckers, couldn't you find anyone else's path to cross?' He then proceeded towards the fortress to continue his mission.

The fat tomcat with a white paw, know as Latthya, and the slim one with a black face, known as Hadkya, had crossed Langdya's path merely to irritate him. They followed him and then stood on one side of the road. They had seen the anger on Langdya's face. Latthya extended his paw for a 'hi-fi' with Hadkya. Latthya said, 'That Ghaari was right! This guy has a short fuse. Come, let's watch the fun.'

Hadkya said, 'I wonder what he told Habib. Habib sits on a stool for hours on end, chewing paan. He is so fat that even if it starts raining, he cannot walk fast. But today he quickly jumped down from the stool on hearing Langdya. Some scandal seems to be brewing. Shall we go there?'

Latthya seemed reluctant. 'Why not wait here? The tea seller will leave now to buy a packet of agarbatti. We can quickly guzzle down the milk in his shop.'

But Hadkya was more interested in the scandal which seemed to be brewing. He said, 'What are you blabbering? I will take you to Mrs Patil's house. The one who has a hairy upper lip. The moment her husband comes home, they both enter the bedroom and don't come out even if there is an earthquake. I have often enjoyed polishing off their milk.'

'But that doesn't seem to have had any effect on your body! All right, let's follow him.' Both the tomcats set off after Langdya.

❧

Deshpande-madam walked briskly. Her heart was beating wildly. As she walked, she played nervously with her earring and mumbled. Possibly, she was uttering some shlokas invoking her family deity. One part of the fort was lit by bright moonlight and the white walls shone like milk.

The dense green trees and the bushes seemed black in the moonlight. The small fortress resembled a huge mendicant with long tresses sitting in a meditative pose. The fortress may once have resembled a real fortress, but over the years, people had scooped away the white mud from its walls to plaster the brick walls of their own homes. It was now a meagre remnant of its glorious past. Someone had once told Deshpande-madam that ghosts lived there. She had also heard from people that the ghosts conversed in voices that sounded like *dung chi pochdung piyang piyang*, or something like that. The very thought sent a shiver up Deshpande-madam's spine. She had been told to turn left at the fortress and wait. She reached there and stood, clasping her hands together, trying to calm her shivering body.

Gengane too moved towards the fortress. Actually, this was his time to go to the bar, gulp down a couple of tumblers of country liquor, lick a piece of pickle, and go home to enjoy the hot bhakris made by his wife. The bhakris tasted delicious with fresh chilli chutney. He would then doze off. If he did not fall asleep, he would fiddle with his wife's petticoat, try to undo the knot, and play with her navel. This was a favourite game of his. At times, his love for Maths would show up and he would say, 'If I multiply your navel with your stomach and divide the result by the calf, what would I get?' Gengane's wife would lovingly bite his cheek. Gengane would then get busy solving his equation, becoming drenched with sweat as the arrack poured out of his pores. But this was rare. Most times he would be fast asleep after the drinks and the hearty meal at home. Today, too, Gengane had been thinking of going about his usual routine, when Langdya intercepted him and changed his track. He walked towards the mud fort in breathless, long strides, ensuring no one noticed him on the way. Finally, he spotted Deshpande-madam's lissome body, which he greatly admired. A thought crossed his mind—not only did her voice have a lilt, even her body moved rhythmically. But he immediately brushed away the thought. He was here to find out if she was having an affair. Lines like 'Keeping in the school a teacher who is having an affair is like growing a poisonous plant amongst the students. We need to throw such people out' crossed his mind.

Gengane walked, keeping a safe distance from Deshpande-madam. She turned left near the mud fort and stood under a tree. Gengane stopped as well, hiding himself behind some wooden boxes dumped there. From his vantage point he could see the road as well as Deshpande-madam. She stood there, flickering a small torch on her wristwatch every few minutes. Her wristwatch had always been an object of curiosity for Gengane. It had such a small dial that Gengane would wonder how it accommodated the three hands and all the numbers. He would imagine Deshpande-madam using the dial as a bindi! Now he was wondering whether she could see the time in the light of the torch. And more importantly, he was curious to see who she was waiting for.

It was then that he saw someone walking towards him. The gait seemed familiar.

❦

Habib-sir reached the fort and looked around to ensure there was no one known in sight. He emptied his mouth of betel juice. At the same time, he was careful to not let Gengane spot him. He was tickled by the thought of seeing Gengane-master and Deshpande-madam's reaction when he suddenly appeared before them while they sat holding hands in a romantic manner. Deshpande, Habib-sir recalled, had a slim figure. He had often noticed the way her delicate fingers moved on the harmonium. He had never really 'looked' at her, but now he realised for the first time that she was indeed quite good-looking. An easy job and an additional income from the garage had made both his body and mind dull and lazy. Otherwise he would not have failed to notice a good-looking woman whom he met every day. The sad realisation about his overall dullness made Habib-sir a little despondent. He was further troubled that Gengane-master was lucky enough to have an affair with Deshpande-madam. Gengane was after all a Maths teacher, while he only taught Hindi. On top of that, Deshpande-madam probably presumed that being a Muslim, the first thing he did every morning was to butcher a goat and enjoy its meat. That was possibly the reason why she stayed away from him. If he caught her with Gengane, that would teach her a lesson. Habib strained his eyes to see Deshpande. She continued to stand alone.

Concealing himself behind some old wooden boxes, he waited for Gengane to arrive.

⚬

Deshpande-madam nervously glanced at her watch once more. Headmaster Dhamale had been very nice to her since the day she had arrived at the school. The fact that she had come on the recommendation of a board member was the reason for Dhamale's friendly behaviour. It created a flutter the other day when the said board member visited the school. When Dhamale mentioned Deshpande-madam, he said, 'What? I never recommended anyone.'

Dhamale realised that he had been fooled, but he quickly recovered and said, 'I think I might have misunderstood. She didn't bring along your letter. It was from Mr Moghe.'

'It is quite possible. The moment Moghe sees a woman, he is more than happy to help. Is she good-looking?'

Dhamale merely smiled in response and diplomatically changed the topic of discussion.

The moment the board member left, Dhamale called for Deshpande-madam and conveyed to her, in the politest terms, that he was aware of her subterfuge. Tears flowed from her eyes so copiously that her small handkerchief was not enough to hold the output.

'Sir, I request you to understand my compulsions. I beseech you. I will fall at your feet.'

Saying so, she actually bent to touch his feet when Dhamale said, '*Arre, arre*. Please sit down. Please compose yourself.'

Deshpande-madam sat down and continued to dab her tears with her handkerchief. Dhamale was silent for half a minute and then said, 'You know the mud fort in our village?'

Deshpande-madam was surprised at the unexpected question. She merely nodded.

'I go there for a post-dinner walk. Once you reach there, turn left and wait. I am there at eight every night. There we can chat and also understand your compulsions.'

So now, as Deshpande-madam stood in the darkness, she recalled the incident. She had no choice. She badly needed the job. Dhamale arrived at eight p.m. sharp. They sat down on a rock nearby. Deshpande-madam began talking of the kind of domestic responsibilities she had. Dhamale was moved. He too bared his heart, telling her how he had lost his wife early and how he had had to raise the children all by himself, from washing their backsides to feeding them. He added ample masala to the sob story. They were both overwhelmed and decided to be sympathetic to each other. After all, they had both suffered equally, though for different reasons.

The moonlit night gently nudged the romance forward. The letter that Deshpande-madam had presented, quite obviously forged, soon floated away in the river of sympathy springing from Dhamale's heart.

Gengane quickly identified Habib-sir in the receding light of the evening. Hiding behind the wooden boxes, he sweated nervously, thinking of the poisonous snakes that may be around. It would take Habib-sir five minutes or less to cross his hiding spot. Even five minutes seemed like an eternity. He began to silently recite the Lord's name.

With one eye on Deshpande-madam, Habib-sir searched for a place to hide. He spotted some boxes stacked one over the other, making a wall of sorts, and he hid behind it. But soon he stumbled and fell. The wall of boxes too fell, making a loud noise. Hearing that, Gengane broke into a cold sweat and quickly made to escape. In the ensuing melee, he rammed into Habib-sir. They instantly recognised each other. Quite naturally, they entered into a silent agreement that they would not expose each other. They agreed that they needed to find out what Deshpande-madam was up to. Having resolved to do that, Gengane went off to Naru's liquor den, while Habib-sir proceeded towards Shevade Tambu Gruha. By the time Gengane-master reached the liquor den, Langdya's father had consumed his daily quota and left.

Shevade raised a questioning eyebrow when he saw Habib-sir. The white-haired old man was surprised to see Habib coming twice that evening. But loathe to spit out the mouthful of betel juice to have a conversation with Habib, he merely continued making another paan with Bhola tobacco in it.

As Langdya approached the mud fort, he turned to get to the rear of it. He had seen Deshpande-madam go towards the front. Since it was he who had sent Gengane-master and Habib-sir after her, he didn't want to risk being seen by them. The rear side had dense bushes and trees, and no one normally went there after dark because it was risky. Still, it was better than being caught by Gengane-master. Langdya steeled his mind to go towards the rear.

Latthya and Hadkya followed him at a safe distance. Latthya was a little tired. He believed that following Langdya was a waste of time, but Hadkya was excited by the prospect of finding something to gossip about. When Langdya turned towards the rear side of the fort, Hadkya said, 'Oh shucks! Where is this fellow going? And where did Habib-sir disappear?'

Latthya replied, 'It's a good thing he's headed there. There are tonnes of fat rats in the rear of the fort, I hope we can catch one!'

But seeing him stop suddenly, Hadkya asked, 'What happened?'

Latthya indicated with a nod, 'Look there! I can see Ghaari in that corner there. Doesn't she look stunning? Hadkya, you follow Langdya. I shall chat Ghaari up in the meanwhile.'

'But what about the fat rats?'

'When I have Ghaari here, who cares for rats? This is a chance to bare my heart today.'

'Latthya, listen to me! You are fat as a pumpkin. Your heart is probably heavier than her. And don't you know she pines for Pandhar Pattya, the one with white stripes?'

     Shrikant Bojewar

'So what? Pandhar Pattya doesn't even have a house. He roams the streets. Ghaari is used to staying in Gengane's house. She needs someone who has a house of his own. I will show her my house. I have a special corner in the doctor's house for me. The moment she sees the house, she will forget Pandhar Pattya. You carry on, this is not for folks like you.' Hearing this, Hadkya ran off after Langdya.

Worried about creepy crawlies, Langdya stood near a bush wondering how he would go towards the rear of the fort. Right about then, he spotted two eyes shining brightly in the darkness and muttered, 'What the fuck! Why doesn't this cat die? Why does he have to cross my path every time.'

Hadkya grasped Langdya's body language and stood at a safe distance. By then Langdya's eyes had adjusted to the moonlight and he was able to see better. He saw something move in the bushes ahead and soon two hands emerged. It was Dhamale-sir and, holding on to his shirt from behind, was Deshpande-madam.

They were both wide-eyed with shock at seeing Langdya. Even Hadkya was in shock. Recovering somehow, Dhamale-sir put on his headmaster's voice and asked, 'Langdya, what the hell are you doing here in the darkness?'

By then Langdya too had recovered and his mind whirled rapidly to think up an appropriate response.

'Nothing sir! My father went to the liquor den and hasn't returned yet. My mother asked me to check if he has fallen drunk near the mud fort.'

'So did you find him?'

'No. He isn't here. But sir, why are you here?'

'Deshpande-madam lost one of her earrings. We are searching for it.'

'Did you find it?'

'No. While you search for your father, look for her earring as well. And if you find it, give it to me tomorrow.'

'Okay, sir.'

Even as he was engaging Langdya in a conversation, Dhamale was trying to find a way out. He said, 'Why don't you appear for the matriculate examination?'

'Gengane-master is not letting me clear the seventh-standard exam.'

'Don't worry. Meet me tomorrow and I will get the matriculate form filled.'

'Okay, sir.'

'And don't mention Deshpande-madam to anyone. You know how our teachers are. They will simply gossip while here I am trying to be a good Samaritan.'

'Okay, sir.'

Dhamale and Deshpande left in a hurry. After walking together for a few steps, they parted. Langdya danced on one leg with joy while Hadkya, having found meaty gossip, let out a meow.

Langdya shouted, 'Scram, you fucker!'

⸎

Ghaari seemed quite happy to meet Latthya. She needed someone to spend time with until Gengane-master returned.

'What brings you here, Latthya?'

'*Arre*, I was walking with Hadkya behind the mud fort when I saw you. What are you doing here?'

'My master has gone towards that side. I don't know what brings him here so I'm just waiting for him.'

Latthya realised that this was an opportunity to impress her. He said, 'Why stand here? Let's follow him. We can be of help if he is in trouble.'

Ghaari replied, 'Come on then.'

They both walked towards the mud fort. At that moment they saw Gengane-master and Habib-sir running towards them. They didn't stop till they reached the main road. Ghaari was a little worried at seeing Gengane-master run so fast. This was an opportunity for Latthya and he immediately rubbed his neck against her to show his concern. Her warm touch sent a shiver down his spine, his claws came out and his ears stood up straight. He had a strong urge to rake his claws against a wooden pole. He was thrilled that he had listened to Hadkya and come to the mud fort. By then, Ghaari realised that Latthya was hugging her, and so, she quickly moved away.

'I am sorry. I was a little scared.'

'Why do you have to apologise? It's natural.'

Walking away, she said, 'Master is now on his way to Naru's bar. I will go home. His wife is alone. Bye!'

'Bye,' Latthya responded heartily. At that moment, Hadkya arrived.

'Latthya, you missed a super juicy piece of gossip.'

'Who cares! Here, I got to take her in my arms.'

'Come on! Don't bluff.'

'I swear! Gengane-master and Habib-sir ran away just now and she too went home.'

'Gengane too? Fuck! It seems the entire school was here.'

'What do you mean? Who else was there?'

'I'll tell you later. I have to go now. Mrs Patil would have left the milk vessel uncovered on the kitchen platform. I can't lose that opportunity. See you later under the light pole outside Shinde's garage.' Hadkya left, leaving Latthya alone, who was still floating on air thinking of the touch he had enjoyed with Ghaari.

⁇

Like a pendulum that swings from one end to another, Langdya's life had changed in one moment. He had always been convinced that his sharp mind could produce excellent results. He felt bad that no one appreciated this sharp mind of his. But like a heavy roller on a cricket pitch, that one event had flattened whatever regrets Langdya had. He thought of celebrating his 'adult life' by going to Naru's bar, downing a peg or two and licking a piece of spicy pickle. But he was sure that not only would Naru refuse to serve him, but he would also pull him by the ears and take him to his father. He had no choice but to drop the fantasy. But he was in a great mood and didn't want to return home soon. So he turned towards the pride of the town, the main road. But to his misfortune, he spotted Bhadya. Langdya was in no mood to listen to Bhadya who always talked about books and studies. He stepped to a side of the road, shrouded in darkness, to avoid being seen. But Bhadya had already seen Langdya and was not going to let the chance go.

'*Abey*, why are you hiding?'

'I am not hiding. And I am not afraid of you.'

'Why are you acting like a thief then?'

'Get lost. You aren't Gabbar Singh. You may be good in studies, but that does not make you a hero.'

'No one stopped you from studying. But you want to roam the market chewing on tobacco!'

Langdya was incensed. He held Bhadya by the collar and whacked him on the head.

Bhadya was stunned, but he didn't let Langdya know that he was stunned. He stepped back, keeping a safe distance from Langdya, and said, 'You go home now. I have told Ajabrao that you forged the marksheet. Your father saw my marksheet and he was surprised that you had got more marks than me. I realised you had changed the marks quite a bit! Isn't there a limit to forgery?'

Langdya sat dejectedly, having lost all his enthusiasm. Bhadya had thrown a bomb at him! Ever since that afternoon, cats had been crossing his path and he had sensed that something was going wrong. However, having witnessed the events at the mud fort, he felt he had something going in his favour and he had forgotten about the cats too. But eventually, the cats had won, and now Bhadya had left throwing a spark at his house, which would soon turn into a raging fire.

Langdya stood near a paan shop, absentmindedly rubbing a plastic pouch containing crushed betelnuts, lime and tobacco. He stuffed the mix into his mouth as he walked through the bazaar. As he crossed Chandu-sheth's shop, he was accosted by Kavthekar who had a harmonium slung around his neck. He said, 'Come now, sing *Jana gana mana adhinayak jaya he*.' Langdya stood at attention and sang the first line of the national anthem in a loud voice.

Kavthekar was thrilled. He took out some coins and, offering them to Langdya, said, 'Here, take these and go home or she may run away with that Marwari fellow.'

Langdya had an eight anna coin which the paanwallah had returned. He put that in Kavthekar's palm and walked away.

When he reached home, Ajabrao, as expected, was wildly drunk. After hearing about his son's exploits from Bhadya, he had gone back to Naru's bar and downed another two tumblers of liquor. He now sat on the tin roof of the house. Langdya's mother was worried that he may slip and fall. She stood in the garden cajoling him to come down. 'Langdya's Bappa, come down. Please, don't stay there anymore.'

'I am not going to come down. What kind of a son have I given birth to? The fucker makes a bloody fool of his own father!'

'Bappa, I beg of you, please come down. If you fall, it will be a disaster.'

Seeing Langdya enter, his mother pounced on him. 'You liar! That Bhadya told the truth to your father and now he is drunk and refuses to come down. What shall I do?'

Langdya looked up at his father and again said, 'Bappa, come down!'

Ajabrao's anger doubled when he heard Langdya's voice. 'You want me to come down? It is time for me to go up! My own son makes a *chootiya* of me. Why should I come down?'

'I didn't fool you.'

'How many marks did you score, you fucker?'

'I showed you the marksheet.'

'Bhadya has told me everything.'

'Do you believe him more than you believe me?'

'I was wondering how you managed to score so well.'

Langdya thought for a moment and said, 'Come to the school with me tomorrow. We will meet Dhamale-sir with the marksheet. If he says it is forged, you may whip me any way you like.'

Ajabrao was surprised to see his son speak with such confidence. It had a sobering effect on him and he came down. Langdya's mother was relieved that the drama had been postponed for a day.

Ajabrao hugged Langdya and kissed him on his cheeks saying, 'Langdya, did you really do so well?'

The strong stench of country liquor hit Langdya's nostrils. 'Yes, I told you so.'

Now both mother shand son knew that Ajabrao, in his maudlin state, would cry for an hour or more. They settled down to sleep. The drama for the day ended in peace. The white tomcat watching the drama unfold in Langdya's home jumped on to the roof of the next house muttering, 'Will Langdya take his father to school tomorrow?'

As he crossed one roof after another, moving towards the light pole near Shinde's garage, he recalled what Langdya had said. He had a juicy story to share with the others this evening.

The next morning Langdya sat down to breakfast after a bath. Dipping the previous night's bhakri into his cup of tea, he asked, 'Ma, has Bappa woken up?'

'You expect him to get up so early? He drank two extra glasses last night—I doubt he will wake up before noon.'

'But we have to meet Dhamale-sir in the school this morning.'

Langdya's mother was taken aback. She thought Langdya had simply bluffed the previous evening. She didn't have any delusions about Langdya's performance in studies. 'Dear son, why do you want to torture the poor soul? Let him sleep,' she said, as she lovingly ruffled his hair. 'You must study sincerely and try to score good marks. Then everything will be fine. You will get a good job and we will all live happily ever after.'

Langdya's mother had been paving the floor outside the house with a mixture of cowdung and water, a village tradition to keep the floor clear of insects. Her saree reeked of cowdung, and when she hugged Langdya, he nearly suffocated. Yet, the embrace felt good. As she wiped her tears, he said, 'Wake him up. I have to go to school. The marksheet is genuine.'

Langdya's mother angrily pushed him away. 'What kind of tomfoolery is this? Don't I know? Why are you doing this? Go to school. You are used to failing and we are used to seeing you fail.'

She was telling the truth. But the events of the previous evening at the mud fort had changed things in Langdya's favour. Langdya was sure Dhamale-sir would not call his bluff. He was keen to check the 'power' of his discovery, the secret affair between Dhamale-sir and Deshpande-madam. If Dhamale-sir were to fling the marksheet in his face and call him a liar, there was nothing to lose. At worst, Ajabrao would get drunk once more and climb on to the roof. Langdya was willing to take that chance.

He went in and shook Ajabrao awake. 'Hey Bappa, get up! Are you not coming to the school?'

Ajabrao got up, had a bath and put on a clean shirt. He dabbed perfume on his body and walked all the way to school with Langdya. 'Wait till the national anthem gets over,' Langdya said, asking his father to stay at the gate while he entered the school.

Langdya noticed that Habib-sir and Gengane-master stood next to each other while the anthem was being sung. As soon as the anthem ended, he went to his father and said, 'Come, let's meet Dhamale-sir.'

They went and stood outside Dhamale-sir's room. Seated on a stool outside the room was Dhamale's peon, who looked disparagingly at the boy. 'What is it, Langdya?'

'I have to meet sir.'

'About what? Come later.'

'Sir has asked me to meet.'

The peon looked at Langdya with surprise and went in to inform Dhamale. When he came out, he looked even more surprised. Without saying a word, he merely pushed the curtain aside to allow them to enter.

Langdya and his father entered the room.

'Sir, this is my father.'

Ajabrao bent low in an elaborate namaskar. When Dhamale-sir asked him to sit, he sat on the edge of the chair, looking around nervously. Langdya kept standing as he took the marksheet out of his pocket and put it on the table. 'Sir, my father feels this marksheet is forged.'

Dhamale-sir looked at the marksheet. Naturally, he couldn't believe his eyes. He took out a register marked '7A' and then, looking at it, mumbled something inaudible. He then looked at Langdya's father and said, 'Ajabrao, the marksheet is authentic. Pitambar seems to have put in a lot of effort, and I have decided to ask him to appear for the matriculate exam this year.'

Ajabrao had tears in his eyes. He stood up and hugged Langdya. He touched Dhamale-sir's feet and exited the room, his arms around Langdya's shoulders. Langdya, obviously, was in seventh heaven. He saw his father off at the school gate and turned towards his classroom. At that very moment, a black cat jumped down from the boundary wall. She was about to cross Langdya's path when he raised his hand saying, 'Please! Let me go first.'

The black cat stopped. She had probably realised that Langdya's voice today was mellow and not vicious like on other days. She wondered what had transpired in Dhamale-sir's room. When Langdya stepped out of Dhamale-sir's room, she was sitting on the wall licking the wound on her back. She observed Langdya carefully. Something had transpired that had changed his demeanour.

Langdya could feel a sense of self-confidence rising in him. His mind whirled rapidly. He used to believe that he would have to work hard all his life, starting out as a helper in the local grocery shop. He knew that while he was a failure at studies, he had a fair grasp of the realities of life. He was also aware that the world recognised degrees on paper, hence he was destined to follow in his father's footsteps. But a single event had dispelled his long-held beliefs. His mind was a clean, fresh slate now, ready for a bright future. When he asked for permission to enter the classroom, Habib-sir replied with a taunt, 'What held you up, my lord?' Langdya looked straight into his eyes and answered, 'I had been called by Dhamale-sir,' and without waiting for Habib-sir's reply, he took his seat.

The event at the mud fort taught Langdya the practical and spiritual lesson that 'Man is the maker of his own destiny'. Not everyone is made to top examinations. If one were to assume that only those who studied well had a future, then just the top ten students would get jobs; what about the remaining fifty in his class? He had often pondered this. Langdya had seen the local journalist—who had started his career wearing rubber slippers and carrying a khadi bag on his shoulder—roam around in a Maruti car. Langdya admired this man who had bypassed the steps of owning a cycle and a motorcycle and straightaway graduated to a car. He wished that he, too, would chart such a path to glory, rather than slogging his way up. One day he ran into the journalist at the paan shop. Steeling himself, he approached the journalist. 'Sir, were you always very bright in school?'

The journalist continued to chew paan for a while, took a long drag on his Four Square cigarette, and replied, 'The marks you get in school have little relevance to life. What matters is how you fare in the school of life. That's what counts.'

Langdya was relieved. The journalist had reinforced what he already believed in. The only hurdle was that he hadn't got a chance to leave the life in school and experience the school of life. But now the 'mud fort' had thrown open the door of opportunity. He decided that he would appear for the matriculate examination and then appear for the twelfth board exams too. After all, for every job, whether with the government or elsewhere, the bare minimum requirement was for a candidate to be either a graduate or twelfth-pass. No one cared how one passed, and that fact put Langdya at ease. Langdya filled the form for the matriculate examination and the news spread like wildfire across the school and the town.

Ajabrao was overjoyed at the speed of his son's progress. The evening Langdya informed him that he had filled the matriculate examination form, he went to Naru's bar to enjoy a few drinks. On the way he bought a snack from a cart-vendor. The cart-vendor would park his cart in front of Naru's bar every evening after making a round of the town. A dirty dhoti and a black cap were part of his permanent attire, as if he had been born in them. His sweaty hair would leave a mark around the cap. On other days Ajabrao would merely glance at the cart full of delicious savouries. But today he was in a different mood. He handed over a one-rupee coin to the vendor saying, 'Give me shev-chivda worth a rupee.' The vendor got into his act. Turning a small square piece of a newspaper into a cone, he began preparing the mix, adding to puffed rice, a dash of salt, some boiled peanuts, diced onion and chilli powder. He mixed everything together with a spoon in the paper cone and handed it over to Ajabrao. As he sat down inside Naru's bar, Ajabrao saw Chiptya sitting in a corner, picking his nose with a vacant expression on his face. Ajabrao barked in his direction, '*Arre* Chiptya, fill up a glass for me.'

Chiptya filled a glass with country liquor while Ajabrao opened the paper cone that contained his snack. He smiled when the delicious smell filled his nostrils—the vendor sure knew how to make a good shev-chivda. Naru was quick to realise that this was a special day for Ajabrao. He was sitting at the counter using a matchstick to clean his ears. The act resulted in an expression of deep satisfaction on his face, as he sat there with his eyes closed, enjoying the ear massage. Hearing Ajabrao, he came and sat near him.

'What is it, Ajabrao? You seem to be in a good mood today.'

Eager to share the good news, Ajabrao was simply waiting for Naru to ask him. 'Langdya filled out the matriculate exam form today. Had his grandfather been alive today, his chest would have swelled with pride!'

Naru was genuinely pleased to hear the news. He looked at the picture of Lord Dattatreya hung on the wall and folded his hands in namaskar. 'Lord, let Ajabya's son pass the exam. Ajabya has suffered a lot.'

Ajabrao was moved by Naru's ardent prayer. The alcohol in his stomach made him effusive, and he began telling his life story. Naru listened to him till other clients started streaming in. When he moved away to serve the other customers, Ajabrao, unmindful of being alone, continued to blabber.

Langdya's father was paying Gengane-master thirty rupees a month, but the tuition had had no effect on Langdya. There was no doubt that Langdya too kept wondering how the tuition would benefit him when he had not understood a single word of the subject in the class itself. But he continued the tuition to please his father. When he realised that his appearing in the matriculate exam and passing it had nothing to do with the tuition, Langdya thought it would be wise to save the fees his father was paying. But then, he remembered Gengane-master's voluptuous wife, and the way she let her saree pallu fall near the tulsi plant, exposing her ample cleavage for Langdya to enjoy. Stopping the tuition would mean shutting the doors on his voyeurism. Langdya recalled a line from the bhajan he heard daily in the morning on the radio. The line 'the flower gardens of temptation on the pious path of duty' reminded him that he had to focus on his duty and ignore the tempting flower gardens. He realised that once the goal was reached, the garden would automatically become his. That evening, he went to Gengane-master's house to inform him that he would be stopping the tuition. The moment he entered, Gengane said, 'Langdya, I am told you have filled the form for the matriculate examination.'

'Yes, that's true.'

'*Arre*, you cannot solve simple equations of the seventh standard syllabus yet, what do you expect to do in the exam?'

'I filled the form because Dhamale-sir asked me to.'

'Dhamale-sir is quite in your favour these days, I believe. Are you receiving tuition from him too?'

Gengane's question gave Langdya an opening cue, allowing his mind to work at its usual fast pace. He said, 'No, he isn't giving me tuition. But he told me not to join any tuition class henceforth. He said I don't need any such support to clear the matriculate exam.'

'So, are you saying you won't come here anymore?'

'Yes, I came to inform you that I won't be coming from tomorrow.'

'Why delay then? You can stop today itself. And you may go to hell for all I care. Appear for the exam and fall flat on your face. What do I have to lose!' Gengane shouted angrily.

Gengane-master's wife heard Langdya telling him about stopping the lessons and the lamp she was holding fell from her hand. Ghaari was watching and didn't like it one bit. She too was surprised that Langdya had decided to stop the tuition. She followed Langdya when he left Gengane-master's house. Langdya picked up a stone and flung it at Ghaari, lest she cross his path. The stone found its mark, hitting Ghaari's paw. Ghaari now stood on three legs, nursing her injury.

She glared at Langdya, her claws bared. She wanted to scratch his face out. She flung herself at Langdya, aiming for his throat. Her anger was two-fold—not only had he hit her with a stone, but also caused the lamp to fall from her mistress's hand. Langdya narrowly escaped Ghaari's wrath, with her managing to leave her claw marks on his neck. Blood oozed out of them. Ghaari landed on her paws and, like a spring, she jumped on to the wall, and from there to the rooftop. Langdya gingerly touched his neck, and seeing blood, he erupted, 'You cunt!' He hated the cat with ferocious intensity. Langdya glanced at Gengane's wife who was staring at him, and then he walked away, limping his way home.

When the cats met that evening under the light pole behind Shinde's garage, the most sensational event of the day was being discussed. Latthya, taking advantage of the situation, stepped forward and took Ghaari's injured paw in his. 'Does that hurt, love?'

Seeing Latthya move in so fast, the other tomcats began to burn with envy. Ghaari felt comforted by his loving words. 'No, it's fine. I was lucky that the stone didn't hit me directly, or I would have become handicapped for life.'

Latthya continued to hold her paw and said, 'That crippled fucker. He wants everyone to limp the way he does. I will bite his fat ass.'

'No! Don't go anywhere near him. I will take care of him.'

Latthya felt a little hurt that Ghaari was leaving him out of her revenge plan. He also realised that she had quietly removed her paw from his clutches. At that moment, a black striped cat with green eyes whispered into Ghaari's ear, 'Be careful. That Latthya is up to something.'

Ghaari blushed and, swishing her tail, moved away a little. By now, the other elder cats and tomcats from the area had assembled around Ghaari. A skinny old cat, who stayed in Kolse Patil's mansion near the riverbank, came huffing and puffing and sat in one corner, pulling a sad face. Hadkya, who was in a mood to pull his leg, said, 'What, grandpa, are you missing granny today?' The old cat looked at Hadkya and said, 'This has nothing to do with granny. That Kolse Patil has bought a rat trap and so I can't find any to catch and eat. After chasing a young rat for an entire day, when I was almost about to grab it, it got caught in the trap. I could only stare at him the whole night from outside the trap. What a torture it was to see that nice, soft, fleshy fellow but not eat him—so near yet so far!'

'These rats are idiots. They see the trap yet they enter, tempted by the piece of roti inside. Fools!' one of the cats added, as if she was saying something profound and original.

After a while, the cats stood around in small groups, chatting amongst themselves. Latthya said to Hadkya, 'I am going to propose to Ghaari today.'

Hadkya replied, 'Get other things in place first. You don't want to start hunting for a proper house *after* she has accepted your proposal.'

Latthya scratched his nose. 'I already scouted for houses, and have identified all seven she will need when she delivers our babies. I will get the delivery done at lawyer Jadhav's house. Once the kittens can move around, we will move to the Kulkarnis'. There is a dry cement tank in their compound. After spending a few weeks there, once they become independent, the kittens will move to the next house. I have done my homework, rest assured.'

Hadkya was surprised at Latthya's earnest preparation. He said, 'Is this your first time?'

Latthya replied, 'Oh no! Do you see the one with the brown eyes? Her kittens are mine. But she refuses to recognise me. See her kittens. Don't they have the same majestic gait as mine?'

Hadkya turned to look at the cat with the beautiful brown eyes, but didn't say anything. He wondered if Latthya was aware of the 'deal' he had made with her. Hadkya too was enamoured of Ghaari; because she was still a virgin. In fact, all the tomcats were eyeing her. But it was the one with brown eyes who had come to meet Hadkya at Patil's house one night some months ago. When she herself proposed to Hadkya, he decided not to chase Ghaari any more. And so, now he was preoccupied with the task of finding seven houses for her and her kittens. He didn't have time for Latthya and his affairs.

One of the tomcats plucked a few leaves from a nearby shrub which helped to cure broken bones and inflamed muscles. Ghaari chewed the leaves and put their juice on her paw.

By midnight, the discussions had died down and everyone started to disperse. When Ghaari started walking towards Gengane's hosue, she noticed that Latthya was following her. Hadkya saw them brushing their bodies against each other as they walked. Then he yawned and stretched lazily. Only he and Brown Eyes were left behind under the light pole. Brown Eyes entered Shinde's garage and, shaking off his languor, Hadkya too stood up and followed after her.

Latthya had already received a consent of sorts from Ghaari when he began to walk, rubbing himself against her. Now she stopped outside Gengane's house for a moment before entering. Latthya asked, 'Shall I come in?'

'Not today,' she said. 'Today Gengane-master has suffered a loss of thirty rupees. That Langdya has stopped coming for Maths lessons. So I am in no mood ...'

Latthya somehow managed to check his emotions and reluctantly went back to Patil's house. When Ghaari entered the house, Gengane-master was fast asleep, while his wife was staring vacantly at the ceiling.

'Is she lying awake because Gengane lost a tuition worth thirty rupees, or because that fellow won't come to this house again? Humans, by nature, are unfaithful. Why do they make a big fuss about marriage? We are better off. Once the kittens are delivered, we are free to go our own ways. One should never wish to be born as a human.' Muttering thus, Ghaari settled into a cool spot behind the water pot and, curling herself into a ball, fell into a deep slumber.

✤

Langdya put a little turmeric paste on his wound and went off to sleep. While he was asleep, his father entered the house and kissed him gently, taking care not to wake him up. The stench of cheap liquor rudely wafted over from his breath to Langdya's nostrils and Langdya dreamt that he was in Naru's bar, enjoying a few glasses of the local arrack.

He woke up late and then went to the riverbank for his ablutions. Once done, he picked up a neem twig and, chewing it absentmindedly, began to walk home. He spotted Dhamale-sir on his scooter and wondered where he was going so early in the morning. Dhamale stopped the scooter when he saw Langdya.

'Good that we met. Here, take this!' He took out a hundred-rupee note and, handing it to Langdya, said, 'Take five kilos of rice to madam's house.' Without waiting for a reply, Dhamale raced away. He didn't bother to explain what Langdya was to do. Langdya went to Jamshedbhai's shop and bought five kilos of rice. To deliver the sack of rice to Alaknanda Deshpande's house, he hired a cycle at fifty paise per hour. After deducting all expenses, Langdya was left with seven rupees and twelve annas. So he walked into a hotel and enjoyed a plate of hot pakoras and tea. A five-rupee note was still left in his pocket. Langdya silently prayed for the well-being of the man who had built the mud fort centuries ago as he, for the nth time, fingered the five-rupee note in his pocket. He couldn't believe that he had earned five rupees!

Chapter 2

Langdya, who was once known as a 'duffer' for staying in the same class for three years, was now an important person. Given his age, he should have been in the tenth or eleventh standard, but he looked bigger than even the twelfth-grade students. The old, despised and ridiculed Langdya was history. Like the small, innocuous black firecracker which, on being lit, transforms into a long, black snake, Langdya had suddenly become someone others could not ignore. Dhamale-sir's dirty secret had turned into a magic wand in Lagdya's hand. Langdya knew that it was impossible for such affairs to remain concealed in a small village like his. So it was urgent to warm his hands while the fire was still burning.

Soon he came to be recognised as Dhamale-sir's 'special' man. Langdya found it difficult to retain the knowledge found in textbooks, but was smart enough to acquire the knowledge, intelligence, common sense and cunning needed to survive in the real world. Once Habib-sir accosted him. 'Tell me Langdya, whom did Deshpande-madam meet that evening?'

Langdya was sure he would be asked that question. He said, 'How do I know? Wasn't it you and Gengane-master who ran after her?'

'Come on now! I didn't chase madam. I was following Gengane.'

'Yes, that is true. But Gengane-master was following her, wasn't he? It doesn't matter who was chasing and who was following. It's all the same.'

'Langdya, don't try to act smart, okay? I know what is happening in the school.'

'What is happening?'

'I know how Dhamale-sir got you to qualify for the matriculate exam.'

'Oh really? It was I who pleaded with him and cajoled him saying I am from a poor household and that I needed to clear the exam in order to land a job. Only then did he agree.'

'Get lost! Don't try to fool me,' Habib-sir barked, and walked away.

The History teacher, Wankhede-sir once stopped Langdya and asked, 'What does Dhamale-sir take to that music madam's house?'

Langdya said confidently, without batting an eyelid, 'She is like his sister, even ties a rakhi on his wrist … but when he helps her, others get jealous. What kind of people there are in this world!' Wankhede felt as if he had been slapped.

Meanwhile, Langdya appeared for the exam. All the teachers supervising the exam were curious to see what Langdya would write during the exam hours, leaving him tense and restless. In the Mathematics exam, he knew that he didn't know enough to even pretend that he had tried to solve the questions, let alone make a show of writing some equations and numbers! The teacher supervising the exam smiled at his discomfort. Langdya growled, 'What the fuck are you staring at me for? Do I have horns? Have you been hired to stare at me?'

Despite this, Langdya passed. He had not written anything worthwhile in any of the papers. He wondered how Dhamale-sir had managed. Finally, Langdya cleared the matriculate examination securing 39 per cent.

That day Ajabrao went all over town showing off Langdya's marksheet. He showed it to a few students of the seventh standard who were passing by. While Ajabrao himself was unlettered and couldn't read words, he had a fair understanding of numbers. He asked one of the students, 'Can you tell me where it is written on the marksheet that he has passed?'

The student put his finger on the marksheet, pointing to a word which read, *Uttirna*.

'So where does it say "passed"?'

'Uncle, "*uttirna*" means passed in Marathi.'

'What the hell! Why can't they simply write passed? Stupid fuckers,' Ajabrao muttered and continued showing off the marksheet to whoever he met.

Langdya's mother kissed his cheeks affectionately. 'Your father was overjoyed when you were born. Today I am seeing him so happy for the first time after that.'

That afternoon, Langdya bought half a kilo of sweets from Bhole Shankar Hotel and presented them to Dhamale-sir after touching his feet. He then reached Gengane's house. Gengane had not yet recovered from the fact that Langdya had scored 53 out of 100 in Mathematics. When he saw Langdya at his door, he said, 'You are terrific, Langdya! How did you manage the feat?'

Langdya touched Gengane's feet and said, 'Sir, you know how to solve equations in a particular manner. But there are other ways too.'

As he was leaving, Langdya left a few sweets on the dining table saying, 'These are for madam.' Langdya heard a noise from the kitchen, and before he could register what was happening, Ghaari had jumped up and polished the sweets off. She was pregnant and had been craving something sweet to eat since morning. Langdya lost his cool. 'Eat, you bitch. After all, it is for you only.' Ghaari ignored his comment and sat there licking her paws.

As soon as Langdya stepped out of Gengane's house, he resolved to improve his language. He had always admired how pure and polished Gengane's language was. He decided that he, too, would make an effort to speak without using cuss words and colloquialisms. Fearing that Ghaari may once again cross his path, he quickly went over to the other side of the road. But the cat didn't come out that day.

Langdya had rented a bicycle for a couple of hours. He still had half an hour left before returning it to the stand, so he turned towards Deshpande-madam's house. He offered her the sweets and, as he was leaving, he said, 'Madam, thanks to you, I passed.'

Handing him a glass of water, Deshpande-madam said, '*Arre*, you passed because you studied hard. I teach music. What is my contribution in your success?'

'A lot, but you won't understand,' said Langdya, pedalling his bicycle.

No one but Fate knew that Langdya's clearing the matriculate examination was to change the fortunes of Ajabrao's family forever. That night Ajabrao sat on the rooftop, singing Marathi abhangs. He sang his favourite bhajan in his loud voice: 'Happiness brings further happiness and that's why my mind is so full of it today.'

Chapter 3

On matriculating, Langdya jumped three classes and began studying alongside classmates who had been with him in the first standard. Most of the bright students had opted for the Science stream; a few others had taken Commerce; and those remaining had opted for Arts. Seeing that his classmates were not much different from him, Langdya's inferiority complex got washed away with the waters of the Chandrabhaga. The river was nowhere near Langdya's town, but Ajabrao was a believer in the Warkari faith, and he called every river Chandrabhaga. Langdya too picked up the same habit and he too believed that every river was Chandrabhaga. The students in the Science stream were immersed in studies, while the Commerce fellows were uninterested. Thus the responsibility of participating in cultural programmes fell upon the students in the Arts stream. And so, when Langdya joined the eleventh standard, the responsibility of organising the cultural programme fell on the 11th 'Arts' section of Shrimati Chandraprabhai Rathi School.

Quite naturally Langdya was made the leader. He met Dhamale-sir to discuss the programme. 'Sir, I feel we must perform a sangeetika.'

'What does that mean?'

Langdya's interest in culture doubled when he realised that *he* was explaining something to Dhamale-sir. He said, 'Sir, a sangeetika is a play whose dialogues are written in the form of poetry. And all the dialogues are sung, not spoken.'

'*Arre*, who will write this and who will set it to music?'

'Don't you worry, sir. Our Marathi teacher Kale-sir has agreed to write it and, for music, we already have Deshpande-madam.'

Godfather is a movie that Langdya may not have seen. But he adopted its famous dialogue, 'I will make him an offer he can't refuse'. He was confident that any proposal which had Deshpande-madam at the heart of it, and which meant that she would stay after class hours in school, would be readily accepted. The moment Dhamale-sir agreed to his first proposal, he said, 'Sir, we must get this printed in newspapers. After all, this will increase our school's popularity.'

Dhamale-sir was surprised as to why no one had suggested this earlier. He suddenly saw Langdya in a new light. He said, 'I fully agree. You know Baban Dhage, the reporter, don't you? Go and tell him.'

'That I will, sir, but he would need some incentive to print the information. After all, if we keep him happy, we can use him later too.'

Dhamale-sir called for the clerk and gave Langdya two hundred rupees from the entertainment programme budget. Langdya reached Baban Dhage's house.

'Is Dhage-saheb at home?'

Baban Dhage stepped out, wearing a lungi. For a moment Langdya didn't recognise him, for he had always seen Baban in kurta and trousers. Dhage stood at the door looking at Langdya questioningly, when he said, 'I have been sent by Dhamale-sir. He wanted the news of our entertainment programme to be published in your paper.'

'*Arre*, newspapers are not interested in such activities.'

'Why don't you try, Dhage-dada? Our school is going to present a musical this year, which I am directing. It has a social message. And we will take care of your "chai-paani".'

Dhage asked Langdya to step into the house. He got all the information that Langdya had brought for him as well as the hundred-rupee note that Langdya folded into his palm. As Langdya was leaving after drinking the cup of tea offered to him, Dhage said, 'I will try my best, my dear. I hope it gets published. But I can't guarantee anything, okay?'

Langdya merely nodded in acknowledgement. He had earned a hundred rupees today. On his way home, he bought a Lux soap, a tin of Parachute oil, and two kilogrammes of wheat. Handing over the goods to his mother, he said, 'Ma, make wheat rotis tonight.'

A tomcat with a really fat neck was on a rooftop. Seeing Langdya carrying a packet, he was keen to find out what it contained, and so he came to the edge of the roof. A little mud from the roof fell on Langdya's back.

An irritated Langdya looked up and shouted at Fat Neck, waving his hand to shoo him away, 'This fucker needs a kick on its backside in order to be shown its place.'

Fat Neck was a little taken aback. He couldn't understand why Langdya was so angry at him. He had barely done anything. By nature he was a decent cat. He was so decent that at first Ghaari had fallen for him but, worried that her kittens would find it difficult to survive in the big bad world if they turned out to be like him, she had chosen to be with Latthya. She had delivered her kittens in the basement of Advocate Jadhav's house, where a lot of junk was dumped. Her five kittens, their eyes closed, looked like little balls of fur. Ghaari enjoyed licking them. She felt blessed by her motherhood. Latthya rushed to share the news with the others. Which is exactly when Fat Neck was cursed by Langdya. Now, as Fat Neck was crossing the street, Latthya shouted, 'Ghaari has delivered kittens. Let's go to the fish market and see if we can carry home a few pieces for her.' Fat Neck happily joined Latthya and they walked towards the fish market.

⟡

The news of the school's annual Sneh Sammelan, the entertainment programme, was published in the paper. Langdya had a photocopy of what Dhage had sent to the paper. The paper had edited the long news item and published it in brief. But what was important was that the names of Dhamale-sir, Kale-sir, Deshpande-madam and Langdya had been mentioned in the news item. Another important development was that now, whenever he saw Dhage anywhere on the road, Langdya would raise his hand in a friendly, familiar manner.

Kale-sir had sent his poems to the newspaper for years on end, but they had never seen the light of day. That very newspaper had printed, 'The musical has been written by Kale-sir, who is popular in the area for his literary talent.' Kale was overwhelmed with gratitude towards Langdya. Dhamale-sir had read in his mind the line 'The play has been set to music and directed by Alaknanda Deshpande under the guidance of the school principal, Shri Dhamale' at least ten times. He imagined that he was holding Deshpande-madam's hand, guiding her.

The clipping from the newspaper had been put up on the school noticeboard and had elevated Langdya's status to that of one of the more important persons in the school. Ajabrao got another excuse to get drunk and sit on the rooftop, singing abhangs.

Langdya was now uninterested in trivial things—school, studies, syllabus, and suchlike. He had realised that it was only he who could raise his own stature, by precipitating circumstances conducive to his growth. He would confront the problem of passing the twelfth standard exam when it was time.

He started keenly observing the way the Brahmin lads spoke in chaste Marathi. One day Langdya sat in his house nibbling on freshly boiled peanuts. Shivram, the cobbler who had a little makeshift shop near Naru's bar, came to the door and shouted, 'Langdya, your father is calling you to the bar.'

Langdya was surprised at the invitation. Why would his father call him there? When Langdya reached the bar, Ajabrao was smoking a beedi, while Naru sat behind the counter, fanning himself with a hand-fan. There were no other customers, and Chiptya was snoring away on a bench nearby.

Langdya asked his father, 'You called for me?'

Ajabrao said, pointing his finger at Naru, 'He wanted to know the meaning of a phrase. That Gengane fucker never bothered to explain. So I told Naru that you might be able to help.'

Langdya looked questioningly at Naru who took out a piece of paper from a box and read from it, 'What does "non-grant school" mean?'

Langdya didn't know the exact meaning of the term, but having spent time with teachers, he had a fair idea. He said, 'The schools where the teachers are paid less are the non-grant schools. The teachers in our school are complaining all the time about their low salaries.'

Naru looked at the picture of Lord Dattatreya, which hung on the wall, folded his hands, and said, 'Oh Lord, there is a proposal from a schoolteacher for my daughter. But the school is a non-grant one. I thought it was the other way round, assuming it meant a higher salary. But you have clarified now. I will reject the proposal without delay.'

The social worker in Langdya was now alert. He advised, 'If the boy is good why do you want to reject the proposal? Set up a bar for him too. He can work in the school during the day and earn money in the bar in the evenings.'

'Great idea, but that groom too should be fine with it, no? I can set up a local bar for him in no time.'

'Give me the boy's address and some money for travel. I will go and convince him. After all, Gengane-master is here each evening. So there is no rule against teachers being in a bar, is there?'

Naru was relieved. He liked the prospective groom, but the issue of the non-grant status had spooked him. He wasn't sure how it affected the salaries of teachers. But he also didn't want to let go of the proposal. If Langdya convinced the groom to run a bar, it would be a great relief for Naru. Naru's house was adjacent to the bar. He slid the curtain aside and shouted, 'Get some tea here.' Naru's wife peeped from behind the curtain and replied, 'That damned cat drank whatever milk we had. There's not a drop left. Can I make black tea instead?'

Langdya cursed the cat silently and said, 'Don't worry about it, Naru-kaka. You just let me know when I should travel.' He stood up to leave and addressed his father, 'Are you coming home or will you continue to get pissed?'

Naru spoke before Ajabrao could, 'Let him sit for a while. What is he going to achieve by coming home so soon?'

Langdya stepped out of the bar wondering what exactly needed to be done for his school to become one supported by a grant and thinking how he could get the teachers' salaries increased. He was keen to get all the information related to the issue. He spotted the cat that had polished off all the milk in Naru's house preening herself. The moment she saw Langdya, she scrambled away. This cat was pregnant, too, and didn't want to risk being hit by a stone.

Chapter 4

Soon, Langdya stopped wearing shorts and graduated to trousers. His upper lip was sufficiently covered by a moustache, and there were many who wondered if he was a teacher.

The only teacher who got an adequate salary was Dhamale-sir. From that amount, he would send a little to Deshpande-madam through Langdya. Langdya enjoyed keeping a cut whenever he obliged Dhamale-sir. Quite naturally the extra income showed on Langdya's physique as he gained both prosperity and weight.

The school's cultural programme had been a hit. Besides, Langdya had managed to get a photograph from it published in Dhage's newspaper. The school's chairman, who was in the photograph, was especially pleased with Dhamale. The chairman's pleasure had a rippling effect, making Dhamale favour Langdya some more, who in turn shared his tips with Dhage. As a result of all this, Langdya's wallet became heavier.

Naru's daughter got married. As decided, Naru set up a bar for his son-in-law. It was Langdya who got the papers for the land arranged. Each experience was making Langdya wiser. When Naru's daughter tied a rakhi on Langdya's wrist, he learnt an important lesson that when one worked in the field of social service, such relationships had to be accepted without hesitation.

Langdya had never been enamoured of those who were employed. But he was constantly amazed by people who seemed to be doing nothing in particular—or at least their activities were not visible—but seemed to be well off. The journalist Baban Dhage was one such person. But after spending time with him, Langdya realised that his aim in life was not to become another Dhage. He decided that soon he would have people like Dhage working for him. Yet he never failed to address Dhage with reverence, calling out, 'Namaskar Dhage-saheb' whenever they met. Once he met Dhage at the paan shop. As soon as Langdya approached him, Dhage put his hand in Langdya's shirt pocket and took out a five-rupee note which he gave to the paanwallah. Further, when the paanwallah returned the change, Dhage put it into his own pocket. Langdya had learnt another important lesson, which was to not make obvious one's annoyance at such moments.

One of the people Langdya admired was Prakash-bhau. Prakash-bhau was always seen in a spotless shirt, which would be tucked neatly into freshly ironed trousers. He was always prim and proper, as if he had just stepped out of the bath. Langdya didn't know what Prakash-bhau did for a living, but he was sure he was rich. Whenever he passed Langdya on his motorbike, the pleasant fragrance of his perfume would linger in the air. On enquiring about him, Langdya was told that he was a 'dalal', a middleman. Langdya knew of one variety of dalal, which was that of a pimp. But he soon realised that Prakash-bhau was not a pimp but a broker who helped people buy and sell houses. Langdya wondered how many such deals happened in the town in a year. Yet, Prakash-bhau seemed quite wealthy. Langdya had stored the question regarding his earnings in the area called 'unanswered questions' in his mind. The twelfth board exams were nearing and an air of studiousness pervaded the school. Langdya wasn't worried about clearing the exams. However, with the year coming to an end, his relationship with the school would soon end. Langdya wasn't sure if it was a good thing or not. He was certain that he would pass, but he wondered if passing was the right thing to do. Should he continue to stay in the twelfth standard? But he also realised that the time had come for things to change in his life.

Sipping tea at Rokde's tea stall, Langdya was pondering his future. At that moment he spotted Ghaari, who reminded him of Gengane-master's wife. That sent a surge of blood through his veins. Ghaari was quick to catch the momentary surge of lust in Langdya's eyes. 'That son of a bitch hasn't forgotten Gengane's wife. And to top it, he has grown quite healthy too,' she muttered. Ghaari wasn't partial to Gengane's wife, for she had seen her hugging Langdya once. But she loved Gengane-master, who fed her milk and bread each night. She was loyal to him and was protective of him. Unlike tomcats, who had sex only for the purpose of procreation, men were always lusty. They roamed around like dogs, looking for sex. Ghaari wondered if she should take the help of a few tomcats and guard Gengane's house for some days. She decided to raise the issue that evening under the light pole outside Shinde's garage. Langdya, troubled by thoughts of Gengane's wife, was imagining her on a film poster in place of the heroine. He walked home, his mind buzzing with lustful thoughts.

✼

Langdya's father may have gone around town showing off Langdya's tenth-standard marksheet, but Langdya was wise enough to realise that the matriculate exam didn't carry much weight. He had heard that admission to Diploma in Education or the Industrial Training Institute was to happen based on the marks secured in the twelfth board exams. Most people advised that it was better to be an unemployed graduate than an unemployed matriculate. It was clear to Langdya that he would have to go to college. He had heard Dhamale-sir mention that the local MLA, Vitthal Chintawar, was an alumnus of their school. He wondered why the MLA didn't take any interest in getting the school a grant and in expanding the school into an intermediate college. Langdya realised that this question hid within itself some interesting answers, which he needed to uncover. When he asked

Dhamale-sir, he said, 'We requested the legislator many times, but he doesn't show any interest. Nor is the chairman concerned one bit.' Langdya decided to take matters into his own hands. Of course with the support of Dhamale-sir. Over the last two years, his relationship with Dhamale-sir had changed. Earlier it had been that of a blackmailer and blackmailee but, carrying out odd jobs on Dhamale-sir's behalf over time, Langdya had become his well-wisher. Seeing Langdya's orientation towards work in general and his sharp mind, Dhamale-sir had started envisaging him as a future leader. He decided to invite the MLA as chief guest to the silver jubilee function of the school. 'Decided' may not be the right word—it was a suggestion given by Langdya and accepted by Dhamale!

Langdya reached the MLA's house with Dhamale-sir. The elections were far away. Quite naturally, the MLA had no time for the common man. Dhamale and Langdya were told to leave the invitation with the secretary, who would let them know later about the MLA's schedule. Langdya realised that the MLA was at home. He spotted one of the lackeys and, taking him aside, he said, 'The freedom fighter Anna Bondre is going to grace the occasion. He is the one who sent us here to invite MLA-saheb. Will you please convey this message to him?' With a wave of his hand, the lackey indicated that they should wait while he went inside. After a while, the MLA came out in crumpled clothes. Dhamale-sir didn't spare any words to praise him. The end result was that the silver jubilee day got marked in the MLA's diary in red ink, blocking his time for the function. After mumbling something like 'please have tea before you leave', the MLA walked away.

As they stepped out of the MLA's house, Dhamale said, 'Who is going to invite Anna now?'

Langdya replied, 'That old fogey is sitting at home twiddling his thumbs. He will be only too glad to come and deliver a speech.'

'What made the MLA come out? What is it about Anna?'

'It was Anna who had highlighted the MLA's role in the malpractices related to the employment scheme. I remembered reading about it somewhere so I took a chance and dropped his name. It worked like a charm!'

Dhamale was surprised at the way Langdya had used the phrase 'worked like a charm'. In fact, Langdya too was surprised. His language had surely improved. Dhamale rubbed Langdya's back affectionately. Langdya could not hold back the tears. He had never imagined that his headmaster would one day pat his back with pride. But realising soon that an emotional man couldn't survive in the big bad world and would simply get relegated to being worshipped as a statue, he quickly resolved to keep his emotions in check. After saying goodbye to Dhamale-sir, Langdya walked towards the bus stand. Journalist Dhage was standing at the book stall near the bus stand, flipping through the books and magazines kept there. Langdya said, 'Shall we have some bhel, sir?'

Looking up from the book he was reading, Dhage said, 'Buddy, I just popped a paan.'

'Come on, sir! Spit out the paan. You can always have one more later.'

Quite naturally, Dhage could not refuse such an ardent request. Investing in a bhel, a cup of tea and a paan, Langdya was able to get his work done. Two days later, the news of the school's forthcoming silver jubilee function was covered in the newspaper. The portion of the news highlighted in a square box was more important than the news itself. It read, 'The school, despite being twenty-five years old, still doesn't receive a grant and doesn't have the permission to start classes beyond the twelfth standard. The teachers as well as the citizens of the town are hopeful that MLA Chintawar will take some steps to rectify the situation.'

Langdya had invested in the bhel precisely for this important item. When the news was published, the MLA was in Mumbai. The education secretary called him.

'What is this, MLA-saheb? A school in your town, that too such an old one, continues to be a non-grant one. Get the committee here. We will sanction the grant.'

'What about my proposal?' The MLA was busy setting up his own educational institution.

'That too will be done. We need more than one school in a town. After all, it seems like there is an education pandemic now.'

The MLA was in no mood to laugh at the joke. He was worried that if Dhamale's school got the grant, his school might get left behind. The education secretary correctly read the MLA's mind and said, 'Your institution cannot get a grant for the first five years. By the end of five years, this will be old news, don't you worry.'

The MLA relaxed a little. He said, boldly looking into the education secretary's eyes, 'How much?'

The secretary replied, 'Ten.' The secretary had addressed his agenda and was now in a hurry to leave. 'Get the meeting organised soon. I need ten. For the rest, you can decide whatever suits you.'

The MLA returned to his hometown and immediately asked for the chairman of the school to meet him. The chairman believed that he need not do anything until the teachers started demanding a pay raise and the parents began complaining about the leaking roofs. Naturally, he didn't have any interest in working in favour of the school. The school ran on the corpus created by the Rathee family in memory of Chandraprabha Rathee. The third generation of Rathees didn't have much attachment to the school either. Two of Chandraprabha Rathee's grandsons were abroad, working as doctors. Her sixty-year-old son, Hemachandra Rathee, met the MLA. The MLA explained the advantages of getting the grant and demanded fifteen lakhs. This rattled Hemachandra. 'What if the grant isn't approved after spending fifteen lakhs?'

Hemachandra stepped out of the MLA's house to meet Dhamale. Ever since Langdya had managed to get the news of the grant published, Dhamale was a little worried. All the board members of the school were old fogeys who had nothing to do. None of them had any interest in education or in the improvement of the school. Hemachandra explained the issue of fifteen lakhs and asked Dhamale for his opinion. Dhamale managed to buy time by saying he would hold a meeting. He immediately called for Langdya and explained the whole situation to him. Langdya hadn't expected his action to have such an immediate reaction. He had hit the nail on the head. Now he couldn't afford to let it go to waste. He had to act immediately.

'Hemachandra-bhai will benefit a lot. Once the school gets the grant, there is a lot of money to be made.'

'But the MLA is demanding fifteen lakhs? What do we do?'

'What did Hemachandra-bhai say?'

'He said he will manage to gather ten.'

'Fine. How many teachers do we have, other than you?'

'Thirty.'

'What if each one contributes thirty thousand each?'

'Nine lakhs. But let's leave Deshpande-madam out. How much do we have then?'

'Eight lakhs seventy thousand.'

'So, including Hemachandra-bhai's contribution, we will have eighteen lakhs seventy thousand. Then let us ask for twenty thousand each of the teachers,' Dhamale suggested.

'No, sir. The MLA is going to give fifteen to Mumbai. Won't he ask for his own cut?'

Dhamale was so confused that he could only mumble. He voiced his concern, 'Will the teachers pay?'

'Sir, this is about their employment. And once we get the grant, their salaries will double. In the next five years, the grant will go up to hundred per cent and then all salaries will be at par with that of government-employed teachers. That means salaries will be five times what they are today. Who doesn't want such a salary?'

⁘

Langdya's manner of speaking and deportment had changed considerably by now. In the excitement that the school would be getting a grant, the teachers had sold off their wives' jewellery, begged for and borrowed money from friends and relatives, and eventually managed to contribute twenty-five thousand each. Hemachandra-bhai, too, put up his share of ten lakhs. Langdya managed this financial transaction—he was a student only in name.

The day of the silver jubilee function soon arrived. The MLA came with his usual entourage. He beautifully performed the drama of falling at the feet of freedom fighter Anna Bondre in front of everyone, followed by a rousing speech. And while the claps continued, he handed over the letter from the education secretary to Hemachandra-bhai, announcing that the school was now the recipient of a grant. 'Today, I have the chance to redeem the debt I owed to the school which paved the way for my work at the grassroots,' said the MLA. He also threw in an assurance to those present that he would try to get permission for starting a college in the school premises.

Amidst all this, it dawned on the MLA—that Langdya was a clever fellow, someone who could be of use to him. As he was leaving, he put on a casual air and said, 'Come and meet me one of these days.'

Dhamale didn't bother to enquire with Langdya if he handed over the extra two lakh and twenty-five thousand to the MLA. It was Dhamale who would have paid Deshpande-madam's share had the need arisen. Having been saved from the situation, he was quite happy to remain silent.

The day the news of the silver jubilee function appeared in the newspaper, Langdya presented Dhage with an Onida colour television set. He took Dhage to a dimly lit bar on the outskirts of town—he himself was visiting such a bar for the first time. It was also the first time that he tasted whisky and chicken. He initially struggled a little to keep himself from trying the whisky, but when Dhage addressed him as Pitambar instead of Langdya, he was overwhelmed and couldn't resist. After all, someone had addressed him by his real name for the first time in his life. His restraint disappeared like bubbles from an opened soda bottle.

Langdya's father was a devout Warkari, who walked long distances for the annual pilgrimage. There was no question of meat ever being cooked in his house. Langdya, too, didn't have much fascination for non-vegetarian food. But on Dhage's insistence, he sucked on the bones and slurped the gravy. 'Ajabrao, your Langdya drowned in the Chandrabhaga. It is Pitambar who surfaced,' Langdya muttered to himself. Langdya's father had never seen a bank passbook, but Langdya's account had two lakhs! Without doing a single job!

Feeling a little tipsy, he took leave of Dhage and walked home in gay abandon as the alcohol took its effect. He was to meet the MLA the next morning. Dhage, whom he earlier considered a 'rising star in journalism', now seemed quite ordinary. The poor fellow was thrilled at receiving a simple colour TV. 'He is a good man,' Langdya said to himself. After all, he had introduced him to alcohol. And the vegetarian in Langdya had been enticed into trying meat.

While speaking to others, Langdya was conscious of using chaste language, but when speaking to himself, he reverted to his colloquial manner of speaking. So in his analysis of Dhage, what came out was: 'That fucker Dhage must be sleeping peacefully in his wife's lap.' No one heard him.

Gengane's house was a few steps away. For a moment, he was tempted to say goodnight to Gengane. And in case he was at Naru's bar, his wife would be all alone at home. When she had hugged him a year-and-a-half ago, he didn't have the guts to reciprocate, but now things were different. Before he could decide whether to go or not, he had reached Gengane's door. It was his wife who opened the door. She was familiar with liquor-breath, but this time the person with the breath was not her husband.

'He is not at home.'

'Oh, I see. Sorry, I will come later,' Langdya said but continued to stand at the door. When she tried closing the door, he boldly stepped inside, and his hands reached for her bosom. Her protests didn't carry any weight and, in a moment, she was on fire. Langdya was to experience a third new 'taste' in one day.

Standing near the tulsi plant, Ghaari kept scratching her claws in frustration. When Langdya closed the door, she jumped to the rooftop and then on to the road. Finding a shortcut along a drain, she quickly reached Naru's bar, where she found Gengane-master talking animatedly about the increase in his salary. He was proud of Langdya and was praising his inclination to work for the welfare of people, despite the fact that he was an ordinary student. Ghaari rubbed herself against his legs.

'Here you are, dear—but they don't serve milk. It's *daaru* we get here, just *daaru!*' Gengane picked her up gently. She looked at him compassionately. How she wished he would understand what she had to say. Her eyes were desperate to tell him what was unfolding in his house.

After a while, she returned home with Gengane. There was no trace of what had taken place a little while back. Serving food to her husband, Gengane's wife avoided meeting Ghaari's stare. She knew that the mute animal had been a witness to her sinful act. Ghaari resolved not to utter a word of what had transpired that evening at Gengane's house. But she was eager to teach Langdya a lesson. Knowing that her kittens would gather at the light pole that evening after having roamed the town the whole day, she went for their evening meeting. But the question, why should such an unfortunate thing happen to Gengane, who was such a gentleman, disturbed her immensely.

⌒

Langdya had not been able to solve a simple equation in two years of tuition. But today, he had successfully solved an important equation within half-an-hour and stepped out of Gengane's house. Despite his drunken state and the exhilarating feeling of having had sex for the first time in his life, he couldn't forget Ghaari. His hand moved involuntarily to his neck. Her claws had left a permanent mark on him. He heaved a sigh of relief when he didn't spot her while walking towards his house. The moment he entered his house, his mother smelt alcohol on his breath and shouted, 'You pig, I was praising you for being a bright boy, but you are following in your father's footsteps. You are piss drunk.'

Langdya could see his father sitting in a corner, smoking a beedi. He lay down on a cot without bothering to answer his mother. He had never experienced such a pleasant fatigue before!

⌒

The cats gathered at their usual rendezvous that evening. Ghaari had decided not to utter a word of what had transpired in Gengane's house, but her mind was restless. Her anger knew no bounds. She was capable of strangling Langdya's neck, but that went against the rules of the cat community. Her own species, those who resided in jungles, were allowed to hunt humans for food, but cats who stayed in human settlements were not allowed to do so, as per rules set centuries ago.

The rules had been decided when the animals had divided themselves into two groups: those that stayed in the jungles and those cohabiting with humans. The feline species were initially wild animals. Humans had just begun to settle into farming and found a lot of their produce getting spoiled and eaten by rats. They also reproduced rapidly, creating further problems for humans. Despite pleas by humans, the rats did not relent. It was then that the humans went to the jungles and requested some of the feline creatures to cohabit with them. The deal was that the cats would kill the rats and, in turn, the humans would let the cats live peacefully among them. But soon some humans started killing the cats. Quite naturally, this created a rift. The cats also went wild and started attacking humans. After a meeting, a treaty was arrived at, in which it was agreed that humans would not kill cats and cats, in turn, would never attack humans. The cats learnt to understand the body language of humans but, in the process of evolution, humans did not bother to do the same with regard to cats, and lost touch.

Finally, Ghaari couldn't keep her thoughts to herself and decided to share them with the gang that had assembled under the light pole.

She explained in detail Langdya's character, the innocence of Gengane-master, and the lustful intentions of his wife. She finally told them how Langdya had pounced on Gengane's wife and how they had had sex. She demanded that she be allowed to teach Langdya a lesson and take revenge.

The group fell silent. In the dim yellow light of the light pole, their discomfort was clearly visible. Finally one tomcat spoke. 'Gengane's wife didn't resist Langdya's advances. She may not have invited Langdya home, but she did not resist him, which makes her equally guilty.'

The cats were split down the middle. The group supporting Ghaari mainly comprised tomcats who were attracted to her. The other group opposed the idea of revenge, citing the treaty made thousands of years ago. They believed that the issue was not serious enough to warrant revenge. When they reached a stalemate, they decided to take the advice of a wise old tomcat, famously known as 'Sadhu'. Sadhu lived in the mud fort. He was performing a penance that had won him the ability to communicate with dead ancestors. In order to let him continue his penance undisturbed, it was decided to provide him with a couple of rats each week. A few cats and tomcats now decided to approach him for advice.

⌘

Sadhu opened his eyes when he heard the commotion as the cats approached him. All of them bent low in reverence. Ghaari explained the affair between Gengane's wife and Langdya and proposed revenge by attacking Langdya's neck. Sadhu listened with a beatific smile on his face. After a while, he said, 'Frankly, it is Gengane's wife who is the culprit. If at all, she is the one who should be punished.'

Ghaari was not in favour of the verdict. Noticing her discomfort, Sadhu closed his eyes to delve deep into the past. Thousands of cat generations flashed by as he travelled back in time. He reached the time of the dispute between humans and cats. Langdya stood in the midst as an accused. It was Langdya who had committed the sin of eating cat flesh thousands of years back. That was the point of origin of the conflict. There was a discussion on how to restore peace. While everyone was busy trying to find a solution, Langdya said, 'Though I am the accused, I will suggest a way out.'

Sadhu opened his eyes. It was ironic that the whole episode had originally started at the mud fort where he stayed. It was a divine hint, which he understood. He patted Ghaari affectionately and said, 'Go, seek your revenge.'

Langdya woke up in the morning wondering if he should reach the MLA's house as invited or wait for a few days. Langdya was aware that the MLA lived very infrequently in town, preferring to stay in Mumbai on most days. It was better to meet him now as one couldn't be sure when the MLA would return next.

He could sense his mother's anger in the air of his home. After all, he had reached home drunk the previous night. She was happy that her son was being treated with respect in the entire town, but she worried that he would follow in his father's footsteps. Langdya refused the usual coal powder and salt mixture used for cleaning teeth—nowadays he preferred a brush and Colgate toothpaste. His use of formal language irked her as it made him look like a stranger rather than her son. When Langdya came out of the bathroom, his mother said, 'Are you going to have bhakri and tea for breakfast or do you plan to eat in a hotel?'

'No. Give me the bhakri and tea. I don't like to eat in a hotel every day,' Langdya replied. He finished his breakfast and stepped out of the house wearing freshly ironed clothes.

Ghaari, who was sitting outside waiting for him, followed. Soon, Langdya crossed the lane and reached the main road. The hotels were not yet open; the cooks were busy firing up the giant stoves. Vegetables were being chopped and prepared to be cooked on one stove, while samosas were readied to be fried on another. Huge vessels with milk were set to boil on a few stoves. After walking for ten minutes, Langdya entered a narrow lane. After crossing this lane, he would reach the MLA's bungalow. Ghaari tracked Langdya, jumping from one rooftop to another. As soon as Langdya was halfway across the narrow lane, she took aim and jumped on him.

Shrieking hideously, she bared her fangs and attacked him. The very sound made Langdya's heart sink. He realised that he could not run fast in so narrow a lane. Most of the houses had their doors shut, so he could not run inside any of them and hide. Ghaari had chosen the perfect place for her attack. Langdya realised that she was taking revenge for his dalliance with Gengane's wife. He had been wary of her ever since she scratched his neck. But now, her teeth sank into Langdya's neck. Blood spurted out and turned his shirt red.

He screamed in pain and put his hands around Ghaari as she continued to scratch him. But when Langdya found her neck and squeezed it, she was forced to loosen her grip. Finally, Langdya was able to fling her away. She landed on an iron rod sticking out of a half-built home. The force with which Langdya threw her made the rod easily pierce her stomach. She hung there on the iron rod, dead in an instant. At that moment, Langdya too swooned and fell down. Hearing the commotion, a few doors opened and someone shouted for an ambulance.

It took Langdya nearly eight to ten hours to regain consciousness. His mother sat near his feet with a worried expression on her face. She was amazed that her son had been attacked by a cat. After being told that his son was not in danger, Ajabrao smoked a beedi while sitting on a stool nearby.

'I have never heard of a cat attacking a human being,' Langdya's mother muttered.

Ajabrao said, '*Arre*, when the whole world is mad, why shouldn't a cat be the same? Maybe she lost her cool.'

'I agree. But why my son? What has he done?' she ranted as she sat waiting for Langdya to regain consciousness.

Langdya woke up with a stinging pain in his neck. The scratch marks on his face were hurting as hell too. The moment he opened his eyes, he spotted his mother sitting near his feet. He groaned, 'Aai.'

Langdya's mother quickly stood up and caressed his face. It felt good.

A nurse checked his pulse while a doctor gave some instructions to her. Langdya was restless with the thought of being bedridden for days. The strange smell of medicines disturbed him. He remembered what had happened that morning. That Ghaari attacked him so viciously surprised him. 'What the hell did I do to her? Why did she attack me?' he mumbled to himself. And heard a reply, 'You stabbed Gengane in his back. Ghaari didn't like it, and the poor soul died in the process of teaching you a lesson.'

Langdya turned to see whose voice it was. It took quite an effort to turn his head. But he couldn't see anyone in the room. Who had spoken? The voice was unfamiliar and it sounded strange. He then spotted a fat, grey tomcat sitting on the ledge and staring down at him. It's him. But how did I understand what he spoke, Langdya wondered. Or had he imagined it? He looked at the tomcat and asked, 'Was it completely my fault?' The tomcat named Latthya was taken aback by Langdya's question. It meant Langdya had understood what he said. He said, not masking his surprise, 'We had asked Ghaari the same question. But she was hellbent on revenge.'

'She died unnecessarily. Gengane is alone now,' Langdya said. Both of them were still wondering how they were able to talk to each other. Langdya looked at his mother and said, 'Aai, I can talk to cats. I understand their language.'

Langdya's mother looked at her son and, putting a blanket over him, said, 'You better sleep now. This fever is making you delirious.'

But it was impossible for Langdya to sleep. Whatever had happened—was it good or bad? Was he mentally disturbed? He had been able to keep his cool when he had deposited two lakhs in the bank. Before that he had not even seen ten thousand rupees in cash. And now, the fact that he could understand the language of cats had really shaken him. Was it a curse for the crime he had committed by pocketing the hard-earned money of the teachers?

His mind swirled. Was he delirious due to the high fever? Did he imagine the conversation with the tomcat? He turned his head to see if the tomcat was still around. But as soon as he did that, a searing pain shook him to the core. The tomcat was nowhere to be seen. Just then, the nurse stepped in and gave him an injection. Soon Langdya fell asleep. But in his sleep, dreams of cats, tomcats and kittens continued to disturb him. Thousands of cat eyes were staring at him. The numbers went on increasing. And Gengane-master sat there asking him to count. Gengane's wife stood near the tulsi plant. In the mild yellow glow of the oil lamp, Langdya finally fell into an undisturbed sleep.

✒

Latthya was disturbed that Langdya could understand cat language. He had heard of Ghaari's death that morning, of how Langdya had flung her in self-defence, which led to her death. She had sacrificed her life at the altar of her revenge. Latthya was shattered … he would never meet her again. Memories of her soft touch and her loving nature flooded his mind. He was in tears. He promised himself that he would never mate with any other cat. It made him feel a little better. He had come to the hospital to see Langdya. He was about to leave when Langdya woke up. That was when the whole drama had unfolded. But he was unable to fathom how Langdya was able to understand cat language.

When dusk fell, Latthya left the hospital and reached the mud fort. Sadhu opened his eyes and read Latthya's mind.

'Ghaari's death was predestined thousands of years ago. Langdya's past and our destiny have been tied for centuries. It was Langdya who had suggested that humans should not kill cats. His life was destined to be entangled with the lives of cats.'

Latthya was overwhelmed. He asked, 'What shall I do, sir?'

'You loved Ghaari, didn't you? Go help Langdya now. Be with him.'

Latthya was confused. Sadhu smiled. 'It is clear that Langdya's future is very bright. No one can stop him. Help him reach the top.'

Latthya left the mud fort angry at what Sadhu had said. He was convinced that the old fossil of a cat was a fraudster. He cursed loudly, 'That fucking old fart—what does he know!' But unwittingly, he turned towards the hospital.

Dhamale, Dhage, Deshpande-madam came to see Langdya. After all, they were obliged to him. They had become prosperous thanks to his efforts. Gengane-master arrived with half a dozen oranges. All the teachers who had earlier ridiculed Langdya for not studying were now eager to meet him. Even the school chairman and a representative of the MLA paid their respects. Langdya's mother was mighty pleased. She felt proud of her son. The number of oranges and bananas they received was so huge that she distributed them in the entire ward.

In a while, the stream of visitors shrank to a trickle of visitors. Langdya recovered well and was soon discharged.

Chapter 5

Within a fortnight, he was fit as a fiddle. He went to meet the MLA, who said, 'Keep coming to my bungalow every day. We will decide what kind of work and remuneration to give you later.'

Langdya replied, 'I want to be a graduate first.'

'*Arre*, that you can manage through a private college. You don't need to attend college full-time,' the MLA retorted.

Langdya started going to the MLA's bungalow every morning.

There was a lot of competition between the MLA's men to keep him happy and to try and gather the tidbits he threw at them. But Langdya believed he was made for bigger things. His intuition told him that the MLA and his bungalow were a mere step towards higher goals. There were three more years till the next election and the MLA was trying to make money hand over fist, wherever he got a chance. Employment generation schemes, famine work, Prime Minister's gruh yojana for building houses, funds available for building toilets under health schemes, loans available to farmers from banks for buying sheep and goats, funds for digging wells for farmers, and suchlike. There were hundreds of such schemes whose end beneficiaries got money as if it was being disbursed through drip irrigation. While money from the same schemes flowed into the MLA's house as if through a tap.

Once, for curiosity sake, Langdya had peeped into the 12th Science practical lab. He had noticed the frogs pinned onto the students' trays as they conducted the dissection. The intestines of the frogs were visible as their stomachs had been cut open. Langdya went around the class. He realised that while the frogs differed in size, their internal organs were exactly the same. After spending a few months with the MLA, Langdya was introduced to other MLAs too. He thought if all the MLAs were to be pinned to dissection trays, and their stomachs were cut open, he would find that though they were different in shape and size, internally they were all the same.

One day Langdya was as usual in attendance at the MLA's house early in the morning. The MLA got into his car and left for the fields. Langdya wondered why the MLA had come down from Mumbai and was now going to the fields. The MLA saw him and said, 'Get your motorcycle and follow me.' The jeep took off. Langdya was about to kickstart the motorcycle when he saw Latthya. He had not encountered a single cat in the past four months. Langdya had forgotten the incident at the hospital, but the moment he saw Latthya, he remembered everything.

'Where are you off to?' Latthya asked

'To the fields. The MLA has called me there.'

'You go, I will keep an eye here.'

Quite naturally, this unique conversation was restricted to the two of them. No one else would have understood anything. Langdya wasn't able to understand what Latthya meant by keeping an eye, but he didn't ask and, kickstarting the motorcycle, drove to the farm.

The MLA's farm, spread over many acres, was green and well irrigated. There was ample supply of liquor. The MLA's routine was to get drunk there and enjoy hot mutton curry. The MLA and his four cronies were enjoying themselves. Langdya too was slowly but surely getting into their inner circle.

After getting drunk and eating heartily, three of the cronies left in the jeep. When the jeep returned after a while, Langdya saw a woman get down. He felt he had seen her earlier. On closer inspection, she turned out to be the doctor at the local government hospital. For a moment Langdya thought that the MLA, having overeaten, was unwell, but the doctor didn't seem to be in a hurry. Walking slowly, she entered the small bungalow built in the middle of the fields.

It didn't take Langdya too long to understand what was happening. The driver said, looking at him and giving a knowing smile, 'Come, let's play cards. At least we can fondle the queen in the deck of cards.' The driver spread a dhurrie below a mango tree and they started playing cards. But soon they fell asleep, snoring away in the cool shade of the mango tree.

After a while, Langdya woke up to someone stroking his hair. It was Latthya! He asked, 'Where's the MLA?'

'He is in the bungalow.'

'Who's with him?'

'What's it to you?'

'What's it to me? His wife suspects him and she is on her way here. She may reach any moment now.'

Langdya wasn't sure what he should do. Could Latthya be taken seriously? But Latthya seemed so confident that Langdya decided to take a chance. 'At worst the MLA will get angry and berate me. Let me warn him,' he muttered as he entered the bungalow.

He knocked on the bedroom door. After a while, the MLA opened the door, looking extremely irritated.

'What the fuck is it?'

'Madam is on her way to the farm.'

'Who says so?'

Langdya didn't know how to answer that question. He couldn't say it was Latthya. The MLA would think Langdya had lost his marbles, and, in any case, he seemed to be in a mood to bang Langdya's head against the wall.

'I have an intuition.'

'You and your intuition. Really?'

'I swear, sir! She may arrive any moment.'

There was no point in taking a risk. The doctor quickly got into the jeep and was driven out of the farm through the back gate. The very next moment, the MLA's wife arrived in another jeep via the front road. She saw the MLA and Langdya playing cards underneath the mango tree. Feigning surprise and pleasure at seeing her, the MLA cajoled her. 'Come, my love, let's spend the night here. It will be fun.' That night, when Langdya kickstarted his motorcycle to go home, Latthya jumped on to the rear seat!

❧

The MLA now trusted Langdya implicitly. He asked Langdya many times how he had guessed that his wife would come to the farmhouse. Each time, Langdya said: intuition. 'I just felt it, I cannot explain how.' After all, no one wants to let go of a man who has such a strong sixth sense and who can save one from danger. Langdya became his confidante. The MLA said, 'If you can keep your wife at bay, you can get fifty women. There is nothing as good as the Indian marriage system. Keep your wife happy first, and then please the wives of others.'

Now Langdya was given the responsibility of solving small matters that involved the local district council, panchayat committees, contractors, the municipal corporation, and so on. He also managed to pass BA first year, appearing privately for the exam. Dhamale-sir would stop the moment he saw Langdya anywhere on the road. Langdya would help him to get some of his jobs done. Gengane-master had forgotten that Langdya was once a student of his and would greet him respectfully. Langdya often remembered Gengane's wife, but now there was no excuse to visit his house. Besides, he feared that Ghaari's ghost would attack him if he so much as looked in the direction of Gengane's house. Thus he never dared to visit Gengane's home.

Langdya had rebuilt a part of his mud house with cement and brick walls. He had acquired an electricity connection and a table fan too. He also had the motorcycle which the MLA had given him. Langdya had fulfilled Ajabrao's dream of owning a pucca house. Ajabrao, who had slept on a coir mattress all his life, lay on a metal bed now, and said to his wife, 'I feel like we are living in a dream.'

'But you get drunk and then climb on to the roof.'

'What to do? It's a habit. I cannot control myself after getting drunk.'

Hearing Langdya's motorcycle, they fell silent. Langdya's mother enjoyed taking care of her son.

The journalist Dhage, too, behaved respectfully with Langdya. Langdya would sometimes accompany him to a hotel, but he never joined him at the bar. The MLA had said to him, 'Drink as much as you want here in my bungalow. Or else go to the farmhouse. But sitting at the bar, there is always the danger of blabbering something. Never make that mistake.'

Langdya was now doing important tasks for the MLA. One day, he asked him to pack his suitcase to travel to Mumbai.

'Come, I will take you to Mumbai. Henceforth, you can manage small tasks for me there. I need not travel all the time.'

For Langdya, it was like a pilgrimage. He realised that he needed to operate on a larger scale now. The town was too small for him; Mumbai would provide the right opportunities. He had seen in numerous films that the hero, though born in a small village, eventually came to Mumbai and settled there. After realising that he could understand the language of cats, he was eager to move to the metropolis. The town didn't make sense anymore. He was also determined to ensure that he forged strong connections in Mumbai before the next elections, regardless of whether the incumbent MLA was re-elected or replaced.

✍

By the time the MLA reached the end of his five-year, self-aggrandising term, Langdya had appeared for his BA final year exam. Latthya would invariably meet Langdya when he returned home from work. He would give him all sorts of information, overheard from various places, which could be used by Langdya to his advantage. After his daily report, Latthya would go for the daily meeting below the light pole.

One day, Latthya said to Langdya, 'The elections are to happen soon.'

'Yes, it's going to be fun.'

'Warn your MLA. His cousin visited Mumbai yesterday and is likely to get the ticket. There are discussions happening in his house.'

Langdya wondered how to warn the MLA. He picked up the phone provided by the MLA and thought for a few moments before dialling the MLA's cousin's number. He spoke to him casually, as if he were enquiring about his well-being, and then put the phone down after wishing him goodnight.

Making the excuse that his aunt was unwell, Langdya got a train ticket booked through the MLA quota. The MLA gave him two thousand rupees, saying, 'I have sown the seeds in Mumbai, but I am not yet sure in whose house here the plant will germinate. If possible, do make a visit to Tilak Sadan.' Langdya's intention to visit Mumbai was political, but he had given a personal reason for visiting the city. He boarded the train that night, holding the briefcase given to him by the MLA. He had come to the conclusion that if one were to get out of a ditch, a really high jump was necessary. Strides of a few feet would never allow him to escape. When he bent down to lock the briefcase with a chain, he was surprised to find Latthya curled up under the berth. Seeing Langdya, he let out a yawn and said, 'I have heard a lot about Mumbai, so I thought I might as well join you. I will sleep now. Goodnight!'

Langdya somehow managed to get an appointment with the chief minister's personal assistant. He had met the PA a few times. After all, this was election season and it was natural for many people to meet the PA. Langdya got five minutes with Abasaheb Bhosale, the chief minister. Without much ado, Langdya explained how the current MLA was doing a lot of good work and how most of the party workers were in favour of him getting the ticket. The chief minister, slowly cleaning his ear with an earbud, wrote something in his diary and said, 'Have a cup of tea before you leave.' This was a hint that the interview was over and that it had ended well.

When Langdya stepped out, he met Latthya at the gate. 'How did it go?'

Langdya replied, 'Our job here is done. Now let's go to Tilak Sadan.'

Langdya flagged a taxi and got in. Latthya jumped in too and sat at his feet. He asked, 'Have you eaten anything since morning?'

The taxi driver replied, 'I just had breakfast, saheb. I carry my tiffin and whenever I get hungry, I stop the cab and eat breakfast.'

Latthya laughed out loud. 'I thought I wouldn't find any rats here. But I found a fat one right outside the Mantralaya. He was quite tasty. I suppose nibbling at those government files gave him good protein.'

The taxi driver was surprised to hear a mewling sound coming from the back and, pushing the brakes suddenly, said, 'Saheb, it seems a cat has got into the car.'

Langdya replied, 'I don't think so. I don't see any cat here.' The driver shrugged his shoulders, assuming that he might have heard something else, and continued to drive.

After reaching Tilak Sadan, Langdya met the party's regional chief. The chief first enquired about the status of various projects in his town and then tried to gauge how the party workers felt about the MLA. Langdya said, 'Saheb, the workers are very unhappy. There has been no development in the town at all and nothing moves unless a bribe is paid. This is the experience of most people, saheb.'

The regional chief noted this in his diary and said, 'When it's time to distribute the tickets, we will surely keep in mind the sentiments of the workers.'

Langdya stood up. 'I am so happy to have met you, saheb. After all, you know better than anyone else who deserves a ticket. I am obliged that you spared time for an ordinary worker like me. The earlier chief didn't even bother to acknowledge my presence, let alone talk to me. You have made a huge difference, saheb.'

Langdya's arrow hit its mark. The chief asked Langdya to sit down and said, 'The MLA's cousin met me a few days back.' He referred to his diary and then exclaimed, '*Arre waah!* His name is Pandurang, same as the brother of Lord Vitthala. What is this fellow like?'

'Everyone feels Vitthal-saheb got an upper hand by winning the seat the last time. That is why his brother Pandurang is going all out this time to get the ticket.'

'What is your opinion?'

'What can I say, saheb? People get elected based on their deeds. Whether Vitthal or Pandurang, it is for you to decide whom you will bless! Both are the names of the Lord. The one who gets to stand on the brick will be the master.' Langdya used the reference of the Lord's idol standing on the brick in the temple at Pandharpur.

Langdya's reference to the Lord made the chief guffaw. He handed his visiting card to Langdya. 'Here, keep this. Let me know your number and be in touch.'

Returning with Latthya to town after four days, Langdya resumed his job at the MLA's house. The MLA asked, 'Did you visit Tilak Sadan?'

Langdya replied, 'I met the chief minister's PA, and he got an appointment for me with the CM himself. I told the CM that the party workers and I are on your side.'

'But our current CM doesn't have any guts. The distribution of the tickets will be done as per the party's regional chief Mr Chougule's directives.'

'I know. There were too many people at his house and I couldn't meet him at all,' Langdya said.

The MLA was a worried man. 'It's a tough game. Let's leave it to our destiny; if I don't get the ticket I will go back to farming.'

That afternoon, when Langdya reached home, his mother said, 'Pandurang's servant had come asking for you. He has requested you to visit him.'

Langdya knew that visiting Pandurang Chintawar at this time was fraught with risk. He rang him up. Pandurang said, 'I am told you visited Mumbai. You were sent by Vitthal, I'm sure.'

'No, saheb. I had some personal work there.'

'*Abey*, my man saw you stepping out of Tilak Sadan.'

Langdya paused for a moment to consider his reply. He said, 'You may not believe me, saheb, but I spoke in your favour.'

'Of course I believe you. Chougule-saheb's PA called me. He told me everything.'

'So is your ticket confirmed?'

'No, baba. He has called me to meet him. But the PA didn't sound very excited.'

'What can I do for you, saheb?'

'Well, these meetings will keep happening. And I will not hesitate when it comes to giving whatever it costs. But all that I cannot say directly, can I? You know these people, so you tell me. And yes, I will take care of you too.' Pandurang made a direct offer to Langdya and put the phone down.

Langdya remembered Latthya. In another week, Mumbai would be a literal bazaar for election ticket sales. Someone like Latthya was needed to keep track of the secret discussions. The moment Langdya stepped out of the house, Latthya jumped from the rooftop and looked at him questioningly. It was afternoon. The town seemed silent. Langdya said, 'I don't know why you are helping me but I have started liking you. We both should make the most of this miracle that has happened.'

'Tell me what I have to do. I will try my best.'

'Go to Pandurang's house and keep an eye on the people visiting him, their conversations, the phone calls, et cetera. Let me know everything.'

Latthya stretched his paw, which Langdya patted in a 'hi-fi'. From disliking cats, to hating them to turning friends— the entire journey fast-forwarded in Langdya's mind as if he was watching a movie.

✺

Meanwhile, the political atmosphere was ripe. Like a clew of earthworms that starts squirming when sprinkled with salt, the political arena too was suddenly active. Vitthal was trying his best to establish contact with the chief minister while keeping the regional chief happy. But Pandurang's phone calls were at the most reaching both their PAs. He wasn't able to make further progress. Soon the mystery of the election tickets and their allocation began to unravel. Some reached their logical or illogical conclusions, thus killing the suspense, while in other constituencies, the guessing game continued. The newspapers were full of speculation. It showed either the leanings of the newspapers themselves or the journalists who were responsible for the so-called 'scoop'. Langdya was in a bit of a fix. He had taken Dhage's help to get an article published, which praised Vitthal's work, thus recommending him as a candidate for the election. When Pandurang called Langdya, he asked Dhage to write another one talking about the confusion among the party workers' ranks about the two brothers. The statement 'some of the senior members are in favour of Pandurang' created chaos.

Chapter 6

All aspiring candidates had assembled in Mumbai and the tickets were being given one by one. Langdya and Vitthal's other supporters were pacing the corridors with their hands locked behind their backs, tension writ large on their faces. But Langdya wasn't worried. Latthya was in the room where the party chief was in discussions. Latthya would come and inform Langdya as soon as a particular candidate's name was finalised. Latthya came out and informed him once again when the discussion regarding the candidate for their town came up. Pandurang had not failed to notice how Langdya had eagerly greeted the chief.

Ten minutes had passed when the regional chief's PA and Latthya came out of the meeting room together. Langdya stood in a corner waiting for the PA. The PA too casually walked towards Langdya and said, 'The CM is rooting for Vitthal, while our boss is in support of Pandurang. It's a tough fight. We must pray for the best outcome.'

Langdya's mind worked at a furious speed and he whispered something in the PA's ears. They shook hands and then, going back into the meeting room, the PA wrote something on a piece of paper and handed it to the regional chief. The regional chief's face brightened up as he read the note. The regional chief addressed the party chief, 'We must acknowledge that CM-saheb is happy with Vitthal's work. I can accept for a moment that the complaints against Vitthal may not be true. Still, there is a lot of rumbling amongst the party workers regarding Vitthal's character, which cannot be ignored. I find it embarrassing to talk about it here, but it is a question of our party's reputation. It is an open secret that the MLA has illicit relations with a female doctor working in the Taluka dispensary. Our party is known for its values, its principles. It is for the party chief to decide whether this point must be taken into account while deciding on the candidate.'

Chougule's exposé of Vitthal's peccadilloes had an instant effect on the meeting. The CM's face fell. He felt defeated. The party observers from Delhi, who had no clue about local politics, immediately cancelled Vitthal's name for the candidature and wrote Pandurang's name instead.

Latthya immediately shot out of the room to convey the decision to Langdya. The list was to be declared late at night. Vitthal sat in a local eatery sipping juice and enjoying a local dish. He was a well-known and respected figure in the town, but here in the metropolis, he was an ordinary man. Langdya sat next to him and said, 'It seems your chances are dim.'

'What makes you say that?'

'I just feel so.'

Vitthal somehow managed to control his emotions. His face fell as he said, 'If you feel so, it must be true. Your intuition is always right.' He stood up. 'I will go and sleep now. We will decide when to leave for the village.'

The dejected MLA left for his hotel, and his supporters and party workers followed suit. Langdya then approached Pandurang's camp. Pandurang stood up on seeing Langdya. 'What's the news?' he asked eagerly.

Langdya whispered, 'I hope you have twenty-five ready. Our job is done. But don't announce it yet.'

Tears of joy flowed down Pandurang's cheeks. Langdya quickly left before he was asked any further questions.

Latthya jumped into the taxi as Langdya boarded it. The taxi moved towards Langdya's lodge. Seeing Langdya's happy face, Latthya asked, 'Who is happier, cat or human?'

Langdya answered, 'Human.'

'Why do you say so?' Latthya asked.

'What do you achieve in your life other than foraging in garbage and producing kittens?'

'Each species lives for self-preservation and to procreate. We are doing the same,' Latthya clarified.

'Then why did Ghaari decide to take revenge?'

'She was attached to Gengane and she developed a few human tendencies. But she paid for it with her life. She would have lived longer had she followed cat rules.'

'Why then are you making the mistake of being attached to me?'

'That is my destiny.'

'Why did that question of who is happier arise in your mind then?'

'You said "twenty-five" to Pandurang, didn't you?'

'Yes, twenty-five lakh rupees.'

'Yes. When there was no concept of money, all transactions happened under the barter system, with foodgrains being exchanged. But the rats were eating the foodgrains and we were asked to solve the problem. Now you use money instead of grains. You believe currency is an indication of progress. But it also makes you sad. I feel grains were a better option.'

'Are you saying you are happy because your means to attain happiness hasn't changed?' Langdya asked.

'Yes.'

'Even trees release oxygen for thousands of years. How are you different from them?'

Latthya laughed. 'You are no different actually. Man, whether rich or poor, takes in the same amount of oxygen when he breathes. But you define happiness with money.'

'You won't understand unless you are a human.'

'So you believe a man is happier than a cat, is it?'

'I am not generalising that. Some are happier than cats, that's all!'

Latthya didn't want to argue further. He said, 'Please order some chicken tonight. I will also enjoy it.'

Langdya took a dig at him, 'Hmm, it seems you too have some human tendencies.'

Latthya gave him a 'hi-fi', but the taxi driver didn't see it. What he did notice was that his passenger was speaking to himself in Marathi.

✑

Pandurang was granted the ticket for the election. He began preparing for the elections in right earnest. He knew how important Langdya was. He bought a flat for him in Mumbai and employed him at a hefty salary as his public relations man. Quite naturally, Latthya too took leave of the cats in Dhanawade village and joined Langdya in Mumbai. Ajabrao and Langdya's mother stayed back. They were not keen on moving to the big city, nor was Langdya too eager to take them along so early. Besides, he was going to frequently visit Dhanawade anyway. Now his family was under the protection of the prospective MLA.

Langdya introduced himself as Pitambar to everyone in Mumbai. The name Langdya carried the terrible stink of physical disability, lack of education and a poor financial background. It was insulting. Right from his childhood he had suffered the insults which came along with that name. He was now desperate to let go of it. When he realised that he wasn't academically inclined, he didn't try to imitate the greats who had studied by the light of public lamp-posts installed by the municipality. He had turned his destiny in his favour and followed the principle of 'you are the maker of your own future'. He had reached a turning point in his life, and now decided to stop Langdya's journey and hand over the reins of his future to Pitambar.

The allocation of tickets and the elections were temporary projects as far as his own trajectory was concerned. He had no inclination or interest in being a politician himself. He had a ringside view of the money one could make in politics. He also realised that politics was a game best played by those who were already rich. Going by the logic that money begot money, it was the rich who knew the path to further their wealth. And to add to it, one needed to be able to accept failures, take responsibility for the posts given and withstand the enmity that party politics naturally created. There were other challenges which came with holding a post. It was better to take a different path. Let others build a dam; all one needed was to ensure that the electricity and water generated from it reached one's home. Langdya was determined to make that happen. Thanks to circumstances and luck, he had been able to make enough money to last him a few months without him actively working for anyone. And if Pandurang were to become the MLA in the future, their arrangement would continue. And if by chance he landed a minister's post, it would be a bonanza.

Pandurang had given him the job of a public relations officer in Mumbai, but the real action, until the elections, was centred in the constituency. Taking advantage of that, he began his 'fieldwork'. He made a conscious effort to be seen in circles related to literature, music, cinema, journalism, social work, and so on. He also realised that he had a basic understanding of these fields. He made it a point to learn the nuances of each field and the attitude needed to be a part of it. He came to know the who's who of each of those fields. For this was going to be his strength. Latthya was part of his journey both as a friend and an observer.

When Langdya's new avatar Pitambar began his journey, the elections were just a few days away. He ensured that the comment 'Pandurang's victory in Dhanawade constituency seems imminent' was mentioned in various newspapers and on election-related programmes on various radio and television channels. He noted the myriad disparities amongst the journalists covering various districts and talukas. He soon learnt that the journalist who walked with a chip on his shoulder in his territory was treated worse than a dog when he came to the newspaper's headquarters in Mumbai. If that reporter filed ten news reports, the paper published only two of them. He also discovered that sub-editors and the power of their editing could alter or distort the reports in a million ways. But Langdya believed that every lock had a particular key and all one required was the ability to find it. In order to find the keys to such newspapers, he started visiting their offices. He figured that if he was to influence educated folks, he would have to use paths that were different from those for reaching others.

Keeping a tab on the cultural activities happening across Mumbai, he started attending symposiums with titles like 'Social Consciousness Created by Today's Literature'. He made every effort to create a rapport with those who were clapping and acknowledging loudly in such symposiums. In one such conference, a retired judge made an impassioned speech on how the concept of a 'friendly neighbour' was disappearing from large cities. In Langdya's village, a lady passing by the house would ask Langdya's mother: Have you finished your kitchen chores? Having grown up in such a milieu, Langdya missed that neighbourliness in the large metropolis. Pitambar decided to meet the judge the next morning to gain a better understanding of city culture.

The judge opened the door just a few inches and said that the person Pitambar was looking for was not at home. Pitambar had told a lie to the society watchman that he had an appointment with the judge. In the meanwhile, Latthya, who had been roaming around the society, came back and said, 'Forget neighbourliness, here I don't see people living together in the same house talking to each other!'

Pitambar thus roamed around Mumbai, trying to gather knowledge. When the elections ended and Pandurang won, he decided to drop his study of city culture for the time being and focus on Mumbai's Mantralaya. Latthya had adjusted well to city life and had made friends with the local cats. He relayed to Langdya many interesting theories that the neighbours had about him living alone. He did miss the evenings at Dhanawade village when the cats convened under the light pole, but he was enjoying the new life too. He was careful, though, not to become too friendly with the cats in Mumbai. He didn't want any cat to propose to him. He remembered, at all times, the oath he had taken after

Ghaari's death to remain alone for the rest of his life. Taking an oath and then breaking it was a human trait, but Latthya being a cat would honour it, no matter what.

⟍⟋

Now the drama involving the formation of the government and the contenders vying for the ministries began. Pitambar roamed the corridors of the Mantralaya wearing a white shirt, white trousers, white sandals, and with a black leather bag slung across his shoulder. Pandurang had put in a request: 'I have been elected as an MLA. Now I want a minister's cabin in the Mantralaya.'

Pandurang's party had won by a thin margin. While the opposition was trying to gather people together to form a coalition government, Pandurang was busy dreaming of becoming a minister. Pitambar, on the other hand, was keenly observing the opposition. But he knew that he didn't have the credentials or influence to take part in the formation of a coalition government. He had barely established himself in the cultural and political circles of Mumbai. In order to ensure that it didn't lose its majority, the ruling party was keeping a close watch on the fence-sitters. Unable to decide on his role in the ongoing drama, Pandurang sat in Pitambar's house, waiting for the negotiations to reach their natural conclusion. The poll results had been declared four days back, but neither party had staked a claim to form the government. Having buried their differences for the moment, Abasaheb Bhosale and Chougule, the regional chief, were busy chalking out strategies together, trying their best not to lose power.

The atmosphere around Tilak Sadan reminded one of a festival. Pandurang was careful not to say anything that would spoil his chances. Lest he expose his ignorance or his lack of experience, he stayed put at Pitambar's flat. He felt miserable about his situation, about the lack of influence in party headquarters, despite being an elected MLA. Meanwhile, Pitambar was playing his own games, without seeking permission from Pandurang, to create a name for his boss in the corridors of power.

While Pitambar roamed the corridors, Latthya was busy sniffing out the latest information and gossip. But Pitambar was slowly getting fed up of wasting time like this. He spotted Latthya emerging from one of the corridors. His face told Pitambar that he had some news to share. Latthya said, 'There is a list of fifteen MLAs who the party fears may be in touch with the opposition.'

Latthya recalled as many names as he could. Pitambar's mind became active once more. He immediately went into Tilak Sadan. Spotting Chougule's PA, he asked, 'I am not able to contact Pandurang-saheb since yesterday. I am a little suspicious about his activities.' The PA made a few enquiries and then Bhosale and Chougule asked Pitambar when he had last seen or spoken to Pandurang. Pandurang was missing; his name was added to the list of probable defectors. Even in such a situation, Bhosale didn't miss the opportunity to remind Chougule that it was Chougule who had insisted on including Pandurang as a candidate.

The battle for power had reached its last stage, and in order to ensure that he remained relevant, Pitambar staked Pandurang's candidature. Pandurang was now a tired man. The frenetic pre-election propaganda, the anxiety that followed till the results were announced and the present struggle for power, had drained him out. Pitambar took along a bottle of Old Monk and roasted chicken for him. Pandurang enjoyed the meal and soon fell into a deep sleep.

Pandurang saw his name on the list of probable defectors when he read the newspapers the following morning. He was terrified at the prospect of losing his post. The regional chief had threatened to take severe action. Pandurang racked his brains trying to understand why his name was mentioned along with the other defectors.

When Pitambar tried to pacify him, he erupted, 'What does it matter to you? I have staked more than seventy lakh rupees in this election. If I lose my post, everything will go back to square one.'

Pitambar said, 'Please don't be so restless, MLA-saheb. Nothing like that is going to happen.'

'But how the hell did my name appear in that list? I haven't even visited the MLA hostel. I haven't even climbed the steps of the Mantralaya. Yet they accuse me of having joined the opposition. I don't understand this fucking politics!'

Pitambar remained silent. He knew it would take a while for Pandurang to accept the fact that his name had appeared along with that of the probable defectors. After giving Pandurang some time to catch his breath, he began his game.

'Saheb, please think with a cool mind. Your name has appeared in the list and in a way, it is good.'

'What is good about it, Pitambar? Here I am shitting my pants.'

'Two hundred and twenty-five of your party's candidates got elected. How many of them have seen their names in the newspapers?'

'Forget all that. What if the party kicks me out? What happens then?'

'Nothing of that sort will happen. Now, if you will listen to me, I will advise you to stay put here and not move out at all.'

'But those buggers must be baying for my blood. What about that?'

'Let them. Don't you want to be a minister?'

'My dear, here I am worried about remaining an MLA, and there you are, showing me dreams of becoming a minister!'

'Don't you worry! When it comes to face-to-face discussions, just stick to your demand of being made a minister.'

'You think things will pan out the way you are imagining them?'

'Yes, just be patient. You spent twenty-five for your MLA ticket. What if I manage to get that back and, on top of it, get you the minister's post?'

'May your words come true. People call me a miser, but I am telling you, whatever money you bring back, whether fifteen or twenty-five, keep it for yourself. This is my word to you.'

'You rest assured, then. Leave it all to me. Abasaheb Bhosale is ready with a new suit to sit on the CM's chair. He is in a hurry to take the oath. Don't worry now. I am leaving for Tilak Sadan.'

The MLA was worried about losing his candidature, but he continued to keep his dreams of becoming a minister alive. When Pitambar was about to leave, he said, 'Take care, my dear.'

Pitambar was nodding in acknowledgement when the MLA suddenly asked, 'I hope it wasn't you who put my name on the list.'

Pitambar didn't flinch as he looked at the MLA without saying anything.

✤

After reaching Tilak Sadan, Pitambar asked Latthya to swing into action and find out if the journalists hanging around had any crucial updates. The fact that the opposition party had not made a move meant that they were still busy holding discussions with the breakaway group. Quite naturally, deals were being made.

But Latthya had something else to report. Apparently, Bhosale-saheb was insisting, 'First elect me as the leader of our party and only then will we discuss the issue of the breakaway group.'

Pitambar took aside a journalist from a channel. 'I have some news, but don't quote me.' The journalist was all ears.

'There is a lot of drama going on inside. Bhosale-saheb is insistent that he should first be declared as the party leader. He is more worried about his own post than about solving the issue of the defectors.'

The journalist considered what Pitambar said and asked, 'What difference would that make?'

Latthya asked, 'How the hell did the channel select her?'

Ignoring Latthya's comments, Pitambar replied, 'Tell your boss what I said, he will understand.'

The journalist who, since school, had passed her exams merely by cramming answers, phoned her boss. Soon the intel was shown as a 'news flash'. Within fifteen minutes, Abasaheb Bhosale was seen leaving Tilak Sadan in a huff. The leaders from Delhi had called and given him an earful.

The strings of power were now in the hands of Chougule, the regional chief. 'If the high command gives me any responsibility, I shall carry it out gladly,' Bhosale told reporters before leaving for his home.

Pitambar entered Tilak Sadan. He spotted Chougule's PA talking on the phone, while holding a bottle of Coke in the other hand. When he saw Pitambar, he waved. Pitambar was waiting for this signal. Holding the phone away from his ear, the PA said, 'I was able to contact every defector except your Pandurang. Where the hell is he?'

'I will tell you his whereabouts but, first, I want to meet Chougule-saheb.'

The PA took Pitambar to Chougule's cabin. Chougule said, 'What is this? Where's your MLA?'

'I will tell you, saheb. But first, you must give me credit for leaking the news of Bhosale-saheb's demands to that journalist.'

Chougule was both delighted and surprised. 'But how did you get access to private discussions? I was planning to come out under the pretext of going to the bathroom and leak the information myself, but the news flashed on TV before I could do that.'

'How I came to know this is a secret, saheb. But just keep this in mind.'

'I will, I will. But now you call your MLA.'

'I will do so, saheb. But what is he going to get in return?'

'I will give him a cabin in the Mantralaya. Now dial his number.'

Pitambar called his flat, and the MLA picked up the phone. 'Pitambar speaking, saheb. Just listen to what Chougule-saheb has to say.'

The MLA's hand was trembling. Chougule's voice rang loud and clear: 'Pandurang, you have to come with us. I am giving you a minister's post and I am returning your twenty-five lakhs. Come to Tilak Sadan tomorrow morning. We have a meeting at 11.'

Pandurang kept the phone down. Overwhelmed by what he had heard, he couldn't speak for a while.

Pitambar got into a taxi and Latthya jumped in behind him. Pitambar gave his home address to the driver. His mind was working at great speed. He couldn't believe that things were falling into place just the way he had envisaged. Latthya sat on the floor of the taxi with his eyes closed, pretty sure that after the success Pitambar had achieved today, he would get to enjoy a delish meal of mutton in the night.

Chapter 7

Pandurang bagged the minister's post. Chougule was made chief minister while Abasaheb Bhosale was asked to head the party's state committee. The cabinet comprised the usual suspects. Despite spending thousands of crores on the elections, the only visible change was that Chougule and Bhosale had exchanged their respective posts. A single phone call from party headquarters in Delhi could have achieved the same result in a night. There was no reason to spend so much money and create such turmoil.

Latthya listened to Pitambar's speak-out-loud thinking as he mulled over what he had experienced and seen over the last few days. While Pitambar was eating an omelette and toast, Latthya slurped from a bowl of warm milk and cornflakes. After Pitambar ended his hear-me-loud thinking, Latthya said, 'You are thinking of what is good for the state. Your vision is getting wider and foresighted.'

Pitambar smiled as Latthya licked away the last drop of milk. 'I think you were fooled by my soliloquy. *Arre*, I am merely rehearsing. Remember the TV channel girl I leaked the news to? She called me this morning. I am going to participate in a discussion about the current political climate on TV.'

'What is your locus standi to participate in this debate?'

'I am going as a political analyst!'

'What is that?'

'Anyone who has some knowledge of politics and who knows someone in a TV channel becomes a political analyst. Or look at it this way: I gave her an exclusive and now she is returning the favour.'

'Can I come along?'

'Once there is a dearth of analysts, I will call you.'

'I will not lie. I will say that Chougule gave you Pandurang's twenty-five lakhs, which then Pandurang handed back to you.'

'No one will believe you.'

'Why? Because I am a cat?'

'No! Nothing to do with that. Both Chougule and Pandurang will deny that such a transaction took place. So then where's the question of my featuring in this?'

Latthya fell silent. He wiped the remaining drops of milk off his whiskers with his paw and said, 'As a political analyst, your future is secured. People would love to hear what you have to say about how idiotic politicians are.'

'Our citizens are all cynics.'

'I don't understand what you mean by cynic.'

'A common man is interested in the money the politicians make, in their abilities and in the struggles they undergo to remain in power. The common man is in a way jealous of politicians, so he claps whenever anyone says anything against a politician in public. This tendency is that of a cynic.'

'What are you then?'

'I am the one who maintains the balance of power in society. A democracy will collapse if the powers that be and the common man come into direct contact with each other. It will be a disaster if the common man's discontent clashes with the politician's wealth. In scientific terms, I act as a catalyst. For two components to react with each other, there must be a catalyst in between.'

'You didn't study anything in school. Where did you learn all this?'

'Those who live by what they learnt in school become cynical citizens.'

'What will you achieve by discussing all this on television?'

'I will fill in an hour of airtime for the channel. As for me, my image in society will improve.'

'You are confusing me. But for now, I can't wait to see how you look on TV.'

Pitambar stepped out. The TV debate went well. Pitambar's acquaintances called and congratulated him.

Each household in Pitambar's hometown watched the discussion on TV. No one was interested in the content of the discussion; all they were happy about was that 'our Langdya is on television'.

Pandurang sent a car to pick up Ajabrao and his wife. Seeing their son on the huge flat screen TV at the MLA's house, they were in tears. After the telecast, Ajabrao went to Naru's bar. That night, he sang out loud a Sant Tukaram abhang while sitting on the pucca roof of his house.

Tuka says he eats
the laddus of happiness
Don't be jealous
You too can have them

Chapter 8

The portfolios were distributed. Quite naturally, Pandurang didn't have a say in that. While he had been keen on becoming a minister, actually becoming one made him very, very nervous. He confessed to Pitambar, 'My friend, I was hoping so badly to become a minister. Please pray that I deliver on the work assigned to me. I don't know a fuck about it.'

Pitambar assured him, 'Don't be worried, saheb. The concerned department secretary will explain everything to you. All you have to ensure is that they don't come to know that you don't know a fuck!'

'That is challenging.'

'Saheb, you manage three hundred acres of farmland. You have shops and you are a moneylender. For such a person, nothing can be challenging.'

'You have a point. Anyway, we will take it as it comes.

Pandurang was given the ministry of cultural affairs. He was baffled.

'What does this ministry do, Pitambar?'

'Saheb, this ministry is easy to manage. You have to attend film premieres, attend song and dance programmes, give awards, and announce grants.'

'Please keep guiding me. Once I become familiar with things, I can manage on my own, but right now I need you to keep telling me how to go about this. Meet me every evening.'

'I am here for you, saheb. Your job is mine too. Just jump into the deep sea, saheb, I am sure you will find seashells, conches, pearls—everything!'

'But there is also the danger of drowning in the deep end!' Pandurang said.

In his new role, Pitambar was busy attending meetings, right from those with the chief minister to the ones that took place in the cultural affairs ministry. He was known all over, but his identity was linked to Pandurang as his key man. He was now restless to grow out of that identity. Pandurang's star was rising, but there was no guarantee that his job would remain if the chief minister were to change. Pitambar was aware that while he needed to keep his current boss happy, he must expand his sphere of influence beyond Pandurang and the ruling party. There were fifty other Pitambars roaming in the corridors of the Mantralaya. But their brains didn't work in the same manner as Pitambar's. Most were unaware that they needed to have a sound understanding of literature, art, society, and suchlike in order to exert influence. Besides, none of them had Latthya.

Pitambar had bought nearly twenty books of poetry, knowing that throwing in a few lines from a famous poem in a speech always added to its impact.

Pitambar's flat was well furnished and air-conditioned. He had a brand new car to himself, but he wasn't yet ready to keep a man Friday or a driver. After all, with Latthya's existence being a secret, it was risky. He had never mentioned to anyone that he could understand cat language. He was keen to take his car to his hometown, take his parents for a spin, and seek Dhamale-sir's blessings. When he expressed this desire before Latthya, Latthya literally stood on his two legs and danced.

∽

The initial days passed in the allocation of the minister's bungalow, its renovation and some meetings of the new government to decide on important schemes. Only then was the ministry's work expected to start. Pitambar's plan was to use this time in between to visit his hometown. When he reached home, his mother performed the ceremonial breaking of a coconut and anointed the car with turmeric and vermilion. Pitambar was overwhelmed. He realised that one needed a family to share the happy and sad milestones of one's life with.

He took Dhamale-sir's blessings. By then his affair with Deshpande-madam had become the talk of the town.

The current society had altered the definition of 'moral character' and lifted off some of the burden of being a model citizen from the shoulders of the teacher community. This change had reached Pitambar's hometown too. Now it was easy for one to decide whether to follow the earlier values which defined character, or to justify one's actions using the definition of individual freedom. Pitambar had used the ace in his 'character' pack to snatch the MLA ticket from Vitthal. Dhamale-sir should have lost his job, thanks to his affair with Deshpande-madam, but he had, without bothering about what people would say, proposed to Deshpande-madam a physical relationship, and succeeded. It was this affair that had helped Langdya become 'Pitambar'.

Pitambar went to his school and enquired about his teachers. Sitting in the staff room, he discussed issues like school, society, country and politics with them. Gengane-master wanted to felicitate Pitambar for his achievements. The very next day, a function was held to felicitate him. The students and teachers gathered in a large hall. The chairman, too, was present, while Dhage, the local journo, compered the programme. Gengane-master gave a speech, singing the praises of Pitambar. While he was being praised, Pitambar remembered how he had changed his marksheet to show '30' instead of '3'. He was overwhelmed by the thought. It was ages ago. He wondered how Gengane would have reacted if he knew the real reason why Ghaari had attacked him. It dawned on him that often ignorance not only helped an individual but also benefitted the society at large.

He then met freedom fighter Anna Bondre. Anna expressed his disappointment at the way society had deteriorated, at how politicians were becoming corrupt and how there was no one to fight for the common man. He became emotional as he ranted, 'When we fought for India's freedom, we had never expected its outcome to be this!'

Handing his graduate grandson's resume to Pitambar, he said, 'You know a lot of people in Mumbai. See if you can get him a job there. There are no opportunities here; you too could make progress only after you moved to Mumbai.'

After sipping tea from a cup with a broken handle, Pitambar took the old man's leave, breathing a sigh of relief.

In the meanwhile, Latthya too socialised. He attended the usual meetings under the light pole outside Shinde's garage. He was pleased to see that his offspring were doing well. After spending four days in their hometown, Pitambar and Latthya returned to their place of work.

⊰⊱

Pandurang was waiting for Pitambar to return. Ever since he took charge of the ministry of cultural affairs, representatives from the Marathi film producers' delegation, theatre producers' association, literary societies, cultural academies, folk art associations, and so on, began arriving to meet him with bouquets in hand. He asked his secretary to note the names of all such visitors. The bureaucrats and the minister were both trying to assess each other. Pandurang was keen that Pitambar work with him as his personal secretary, but he knew that Pitambar's scope of influence as well as his ambitions were much larger. He requested Pitambar to stay with him until he found his feet in the ministry. Pitambar readily agreed. A person who had never held in hand the Sunday newspaper's supplements, whose reading was restricted to glancing at the words of a prayer, and who had no clue if Chandrakant-Suryakant were the names of famous actors or of local wrestlers—had been given the charge of the ministry of cultural affairs. The government was neither concerned nor aware that the ministry had a decisive role to play in the social dynamics of the state. There was thus no question of the chief minister having a discussion on the subject with Pandurang. On the other hand, Chief Minister Chougule would spend hours conferring with the finance minister, the home minister and the minister responsible for public works. He had called Pitambar many times for meetings, but his contact with Pandurang was for namesake only. When Pandurang expressed his disappointment, Pitambar advised, 'This is the time to show that the ministry means something. This is your chance to do something remarkable.' Pandurang hadn't the foggiest what this 'remarkable' stuff could be. Pitambar assured him. 'Let me set things right.'

He decided to arrange meetings one by one with those who had welcomed the minister with bouquets. The bureaucrats were quite pleased to see that their minister wasn't happy with the CM and in shallow waters about the ministry's workings. But their pleasure was short-lived, thanks to Pitambar's intervention. One may not have knowledge about films, but most people are attracted to the film industry in general. Pitambar decided to first hold meetings with people from the Hindi and the Marathi film industries. It was low-hanging fruit. Pandurang was tickled at being addressed as 'sir' by the stars and film directors whom he had seen only on screen till then. It was only Pitambar who noticed how a shiver of excitement went through Pandurang's body when a beautiful film actress shook hands with him. Her perfume rushed up his nostrils and he took a deep breath, enjoying the evanescent moment. The actress had left her hair loose. Each strand of it was, in its own silky independence, flowing gracefully over her shoulders. But Pandurang, who owned a few grocery stores, could only think of the analogy of how well-cooked basmati rice grains didn't stick to each other and stood independently!

A huge, bald film producer said, 'Sir, our biggest problem is piracy. Please find a solution to this menace.'

Pandurang was alert. Using his native intelligence he countered, 'You know the problem and its solution. Just tell me what you expect me to do. I will do that.' Pandurang had answered the question giving the right pause and in very good Hindi. He glanced at Pitambar who gave him a thumbs-up—'You're on the right sht track, sir. You can accelerate!'

A smart-looking executive from the group put forth a file on the table. Pandurang glanced through the pages and gave it to Pitambar.

The producer who had spoken earlier said, 'Sir, the Hindi film industry gives crores of revenue to the government, but the government doesn't pay any attention to it.'

This was a bouncer for Pandurang. '*Arre*, who doesn't give attention? Not just the government, the whole society is engaged with you.' He glanced at Pitambar and whispered, 'That good-looking one simply smiles; she is not saying a word.'

'She is here merely as a decorative piece, saheb. Doesn't understand a word of what's being discussed. You ask these guys to leave now. Otherwise they won't know what to say and you won't understand a word either.'

Pandurang said, 'Let me read this and get back to you.' The group got up and took the minister's leave with smiling faces. Pandurang was hoping to shake hands with the good-looking actress once more and she didn't disappoint him. Pandurang was once more drowned in the pleasant cloud of perfume that she left behind as she walked away.

❦

The Marathi film producers' delegation arrived after lunch time. What an amazing contrast to the Hindi film delegation this group was. The Hindi group was comprised of fair-skinned, well turned-out people, while the Marathi delegation had a servile expression on their faces as they entered. The Hindi group had felt that addressing the minister as 'sir' was the appropriate etiquette, while the Marathi group decided that 'saheb' would be a humbler way to address him.

The usual introductions were done. There were two ladies in the group and Pandurang noticed that they didn't seem any different from the women he met on a daily basis. Their hair reminded him of cheap basmati rice which became lumpy when cooked unlike the high-quality variety whose each grain remained delightfully separate.

One member of the delegation rose and began his speech. 'The government has always been supportive of our industry. As saheb's knowledge of culture is deep, we are confident that he will continue to support us.'

Everyone clapped.

Pandurang thanked them and asked, 'Tell me, what are your problems?'

'Saheb, we don't have enough viewership.'

'Saheb, the rentals for the cinema halls are too high.'

'Spending money on advertisements is something which is a burden on the industry.'

'Production costs have shot up.'

Pandurang was confused. He had very little knowledge of the film industry and he was almost illiterate when it came to Marathi cinema. He wondered if the government was putting obstacles in the way of Marathi filmmaking and production. He felt sorry for them. He said, his voice tinged with emotion, 'Oh, this is gross injustice. I am a mere businessman. All I can advise is that if the shop doesn't make a profit, one must shut it down. If Marathi films don't make money, don't produce them. I can assure you that the government will not penalise you.'

They were shocked by Pandurang's comments. They were not prepared for his practical advice, and confusion was writ large on their faces. One of them finally dared to speak up. 'We didn't mean that, saheb. After all, shouldn't our culture and Marathi cinema stay alive?'

Pandurang realised that he had missed the point. He said, 'Tell me, what do you expect from me?'

'Until now, the government has been giving fifteen lakhs as grant for each Marathi film. We are proposing that the amount be increased to twenty-five lakhs.'

Pandurang was taken aback. 'Don't tell me! The government has been giving fifteen lakhs? And when do you return it?'

'It is not to be returned. It is a grant.'

'Oh, I see! So do you give any rights to the government in lieu of that?'

That stumped the group for a while until one of them responded, 'It is the duty of the government to ensure that the Marathi film industry survives. The grant is given with that intention.'

'I see! How much does it take to produce one movie?'

'At least twenty-five lakhs.'

'And your wish is that the entire amount should be subsidised by the government. Why not ask my department to make the movies instead?'

The delegation was distressed by the minister's words. Pitambar stepped in, 'Saheb, it is the objective of our ministry to help. We give the industry a grant and they help us with various cultural initiatives. The Hindi filmwallahs don't come forward when we need support, but the Marathi film industry does.'

The delegation felt a little relieved by Pitambar's intervention. Pandurang realised that he had probably not understood the problems and demands of the delegation. He had been subdued in the presence of the representatives of the Hindi film industry, while here he was unnecessarily whipping the Marathi delegation. Changing his tone, he said, 'I understand that there is a need to save the Marathi film industry from dying. I am trying to get a grip of the entire issue. I agree with your demand. We will consider raising the grant.'

Pitambar interjected, 'We shall send the proposal with our recommendation to the CM. After all, we need approvals from the finance ministry. We shall let you know the outcome. Please be in touch.'

The delegation breathed a sigh of relief and took the minister's leave.

❦

A filmmaker came separately with a proposal to make a movie series on the great social reformers of Maharashtra. He needed nine crores.

Pitambar explained to the minister why such a proposal was worth considering.

'This is an effort to repay the debt we owe these great men who dedicated their lives to the cause of social reform,' the filmmaker made his pitch.

Pandurang muttered, looking at Pitambar, 'What is this guy saying? I don't understand a word of it; how the hell will anyone watch the movies he makes?'

After the filmmaker left, Pitambar explained patiently, 'Saheb, such ambitious projects are to our benefit. No one will question how much money was spent on movies about social reformers. And how does it matter if the movie is watched by people or not? Such movies are not criticised by the journalists either. They don't want to hurt the sentiments of people. After all, the movie series is about social reformers.'

The only thing Pandurang could surmise was that he had a chance to earn money. Gradually, he was becoming well-versed with the workings of the ministry. He was busy giving the clap for the 'muhurat' shots of movies, publishing sound bytes, attending film premieres, and so on. Pandurang managed to recover the money he had spent on his elections within a month itself. He also experienced the sweet and romantic smell of top-quality 'basmati rice' in his bedroom. He realised that the department of cultural affairs was quite different from the others. Culture and affairs were two separate things. He was now enjoying his job.

❧

Pitambar's social status was improving slowly but surely. He helped Pandurang for two months in his ministry. But now he was spending his time hobnobbing with industrialists, the chief minister, editors of newspapers, leaders of all parties, and those holding important positions in social and cultural circles. Now, as new doors of success opened, he didn't have to work hard all the time. His sharp brain wasn't challenged much.

There were people willing to pay for the right efforts. There were also people who were willing to do the work if compensated adequately. They were willing to use their powers. It was Pitambar's job to get the two kinds of people together and earn his commission. He didn't have to invest any money in his enterprise. At times he was reminded of Prakash-bhau from his hometown, the broker whose job it was to get house sellers and buyers together. Only in Mumbai did Pitambar learn that such a person was called a real estate agent.

But those like Pitambar who had risen from difficult circumstances and learnt the hard way looked for continued success. Those working in newspapers and news channels would get fidgety if the political climate was calm and devoid of drama. The government was stable and the opposition was inactive. In such a dull situation, a girl from a news channel called Pitambar. 'What's up? No news?'

'Yes, madam. There's nothing to report.'

'I heard something about our CM.'

'Tchah! Nothing dramatic is expected to happen till Bhosale-saheb is in control of the party.'

'I am not talking of political news. I have heard that he is spending his nights elsewhere.'

'What is new about that, madam? Do you know where your channel's boss spends his nights?'

'That can't make news. But if the CM does it, then it surely makes for a juicy headline.'

Pitambar recalled who this girl was. She came from a rich family and spoke English fluently. She always showed off her curvaceous figure by wearing tight T-shirts and jeans. Pitambar suddenly had a strong urge to meet her. He said, 'Meet me tomorrow. And bring your boss along.'

The next morning the bombshell news anchor came along with her boss. They began their talk over a pizza. Pitambar had forgotten her name. He learnt it again during the course of the conversation: Prachi.

Prachi's boss was expecting Pitambar to spill the beans about the CM's affairs. Sensing his eagerness, Pitambar tossed a bomb at them: 'I will give you a videotape of the CM's dalliance.'

'What! You mean his night romps?'

'Yes!'

'Come on! Do you really mean it?'

'Yes. How much are you willing to spend?'

The man who had come along with Prachi ranked, in reality, no higher than a head clerk in the channel's hierarchy. He rang up the office, and within ten minutes, a vehicle arrived. The three of them left in that car. Pitambar later met someone alone and the deal was closed at ten lakhs. Money first, tape later.

The CM wasn't free to have fun every night. Pitambar had to wait nearly a month for the right opportunity. Finally, one evening, the CM got some time off and went to his secret rendezvous. Pitambar tied a micro camera to Latthya's neck and sent him in hot pursuit.

It was sheer torture for Latthya, who had vowed to never indulge in any sexual activity since the death of Ghaari, to snoop on the CM. He sat near the TV with his eyes closed while the CM was busy tiring himself out.

At two in the morning, Pitambar received Prachi's phone call. 'You got it?'

Pitambar acknowledged that the cat was in the bag. Prachi could not hold back her curiosity and hailed a taxi to reach Pitambar's flat. She had to see the recording for herself. She was totally unfazed by what she saw and heard on the tape. Devoid of any sort of reaction, she watched as if they were watching a cricket match, and then, once the tape was over, she kissed Pitambar on his cheek.

She called up her home to say that she wasn't planning to return that night. She had decided to stay back at Pitambar's without bothering to ask for his permission. Pitambar let her sleep in the bedroom while he curled up on the sofa in the drawing room. After a while, Prachi came into the drawing room after switching off the bedroom light. She was stark naked. Pitambar woke up looking dazed and slightly shocked. She said, 'Now don't say you don't want it.'

Pitambar drowned in the beautiful perfume she wore.

When he woke up, Prachi had left. Latthya too was missing. It was the first time that Latthya had left before his waking up.

That morning Pitambar called the CM's PA for an appointment even before breakfast. By now, even Chougule-saheb knew that if Pitambar mentioned that a meeting was urgent, it was to be treated with seriousness. After all, in politics, one had to take care of such people. Pitambar would refer to himself as a catalyst. It was a word Chougule loved. One day he asked Pitambar, 'I like what you call yourself. But what exactly does it mean?'

'Any chemical reaction needs a catalyst to spark it. But once the reaction is over, the catalyst separates itself. To cite an example, *you* gave a ticket to Pandurang saheb, but it was I who got the deal done. Thus I was the catalyst. I merely took a fee for getting the job done.'

Chougule was amused to have learnt the definition and explanation. He said, with a twinkle in his eye, 'Pitambar, you did the job of a catalyst to get Pandurang the minister's job and gained twenty-five lakhs in the process!'

For a moment Pitambar was stumped. He said, recovering fast, 'You too, I am sure, must have kept your satellites in the sky. After all, you are running such a big government. I cannot hide anything from you, can I?'

Chougule extended his palm for a 'hi-fi' and said, 'Well, I have to meet another type of catalyst now. To ensure that the government runs smoothly, I have to keep a few beautiful catalysts handy for happiness' sake.'

Pitambar was driving his car as he recalled the CM's words. But he felt a little uneasy without Latthya. He knew that Latthya's role in his success was undeniable; he relied as much on Latthya's intelligence as he did on his own. On one hand, Ghaari had nearly killed him, and on the other, Latthya had ensured his prosperity and success. He wondered what karmic connection he had with the cat species. He had never tried to test if he only understood Latthya or all cats. But where was Latthya? Why did he leave? Had he left him forever? These questions were troubling him. But he couldn't afford to get agitated. He had an important meeting with Chougule.

He reached the CM's bungalow. The security guard knew him well and waved his car inside. The CM was getting ready after his breakfast to meet the common citizens. He welcomed Pitambar with a smile and said, 'Come in, Mr Catalyst. What brings you here so early in the morning?'

Pitambar picked up a TV remote kept on a table nearby and switched on the TV. He browsed through the menu and stopped at a specific channel. The headlines in bold letters screamed, 'Explosive scandal to break tonight. Watch exclusively on this channel.'

The CM smiled and said, 'These guys have made it a habit to call everything explosive. They are not interested in covering normal events.'

Pitambar got to the point immediately. 'I have come to discuss this only. The scandal they are talking about involves you.'

The CM was stumped. He was at a loss. He wondered what the news channel had on him. He asked Pitambar, 'Do you know what this is about?'

'Yes. That is why I am here. I know a girl in the TV channel. I got the scoop from her.'

'What is it?'

'They have your rendezvous with one of your lady catalysts on tape.'

'Impossible! How did they get that?'

'How would I know?'

Chougule called for his PA. He asked him to get the channel head to his house urgently. Within an hour, a posh car arrived at the CM's bungalow and a well-dressed, plump Bengali gentleman stepped out.

He entered the bungalow, and the moment he saw the CM, he put the tape on the table and said, apologising profusely, 'I have sacked the culprit already, sir. It was a big mistake.'

'Have you kept a copy of this?' Chougule glared questioningly.

The Bengali gentleman looked down and said, 'Sir, you may whack me if you want. I won't dare do that. I have to live in this city under your command.'

The channel head left. The CM went out to attend the janata durbar with a relieved expression on his face. He didn't forget to thank Pitambar before leaving. 'Your network seems to be stronger than my satellites, Mr Catalyst! I owe you one. At the appropriate time, I shall pay you back.'

Pitambar went out as the janata durbar began. As he was about to start his car, a pair of breasts peeped in, followed by Prachi's face. She said, glaring at him, 'Clever guy you are!'

Pitambar pretended not to have heard her and asked, 'Shall I drop you somewhere?'

'No! If anyone from my channel sees me with you, I will lose my job. One person has already lost his.'

'You guys are all sophisticated Dhages. Your channel should be named Dhage Channel.'

Prachi looked at him, confused. What was he saying?

'Now what's this Dhage?' she asked.

In response, Pitambar merely waved his hand and drove away.

✣

Pitambar had ten lakhs in his bank. Additionally, he had Chougule's assurance to redeem the debt whenever he wanted. It had been a great start to the day. But he was worried about Latthya. To while away some time, he drove towards Pandurang's office.

The minister was happy to see Pitambar. He was quite well adjusted in his ministry now. He had learnt the art of making money while putting on an act of working for cultural upliftment. As Pitambar entered, he saw a famous poet and a rookie poetess sitting with the minister. Pandurang introduced them to Pitambar. The poet was happy to meet Pitambar as he too was a 'catalyst' in his own field. Homogenous poles may stay apart but know each other well! The poetess was new to the game and reacted to every statement. Her nervousness was apparent as she dabbed her face with her tiny handkerchief every five minutes.

'She wants her collection of poems to be released. I am asking our literature committee to look into it,' the minister informed Pitambar.

'*Arre waah!* What's the title of your collection?' Pitambar asked.

Hoping that the newbie would answer the question, the poet looked in her direction. She was a little confused. She didn't know how to react. She wasn't aware of the clout Pitambar had in the ministry. She looked askance at the poet who nodded. It was a hint for her to answer. She cleared her throat to gather her thoughts and said, '*Stone Pestle*. It is the title of the first poem in the book and I thought that was what I would name the collection.'

'*Waah*, very nice,' Pitambar said.

'The title itself suggests that the collection is that of a poetess, doesn't it?' Minister Pandurang, who was by now habituated to these type of situations, said. On hearing this, the poetess happily said, 'Yes, the stone and pestle—they represent women and the kind of pressures they are subjected to by chauvinistic men. Another interpretation is about the way women have been caught in the stone-pestle over centuries. In other words ...'

The poetess would have continued to wax eloquent, peeling away further layers of meaning, but a slight nudge from the poet on her toe warned her to stop. Pitambar noticed that but didn't say anything.

Worried that the lady may now read out her entire collection, Pandurang quickly added a note of appreciation and gushed, '*Waah, waah!*'

He then looked at the poet and said, 'There has to be an outlet for women's angst. Let the book get published. I will instruct the committee.'

The poet was happy to receive the minister's vote. He said, 'Shall I call the committee secretary?' Without waiting for the minister's answer, he dialled the number.

'Namaskar, Khirade-saheb. The minister wants to have a word with you,' he said, handing the phone to the minister.

'Khirade-saheb, how are things?'

'Everything's fine, saheb.'

'We must promote the womenfolk. After all, that is our true culture. Right from Ramrajya onwards. After all, Lord Ram began by redeeming Ahalya from her curse. We need to take the Lord's cause further.'

'Yes, saheb.'

'We have a poetess here, Sanjivani Ghoghare. I am sending you her collection, *Stone Pestle*. Get it published.'

'Sure, saheb. I need to discuss a few other things with you.'

'Why don't you come down here? Any day is fine, Khirade-saheb. We shall discuss,' the minister said, keeping the phone down.

The flower and the butterfly said their 'thanks' and left. Pitambar was surprised at the way Pandurang had grown into his role.

'*Waah*, saheb. You are running at top speed!'

'*Arre*, baba, the very fact that one is holding a cricket bat forces one to learn the game. One may get out a few times, but eventually the batsman will learn to hit a boundary.'

Pitambar was meeting the minister after a long gap. He was thus aware that he would not be allowed to go unless he had an elaborate lunch. Latthya's absence was troubling him, so he thought it better to spend some time with Pandurang. That would take his mind off Latthya for a while at least.

Pandurang took Pitambar to his bungalow. The minister had recently been to his constituency. Pitambar got an update on his town. But the minister was more keen to hear the latest from Pitambar. He knew that Pitambar always had some classified information up his sleeve. He asked, 'So what is the CM up to?'

'Things are going very well for him.'

'What happened this morning?'

'Morning? Nothing, why? I was there at his bungalow, in fact.'

'That is why I am asking you?'

'Nothing special.'

'Well, don't tell me if you don't wish to. But who was the bombshell in the tape, then?'

One may wonder what benefit the common people derived from the 'right to information', but Pitambar knew how to extract information and secure his rights while being in politics. Pitambar knew there was no point in hiding. He said, 'You know her, saheb.'

'Why don't you tell me her name, then?'

When Pitambar gave him the information, the minister said, 'I see! Now that she is the CM's "stone and pestle", I'd better stay away from her. I wanted to know her name so that I could keep my distance.'

The minister didn't want Pitambar to leave so early. After all, it was only Pitambar who understood him well.

Chapter 9

Pitambar's stature continued to grow. He neither represented a party nor a person. He continued on his own onward journey, carefully hiding the scandalous secrets of many persons. Gengane-master had not succeeded in teaching him how mathematical equations worked, but the school of life had taught Pitambar which secrets needed to be stored away permanently and which ones were to be used, and when. He had realised that one needed to solve the equations of life oneself.

An impressive collection of books could be found in Pitambar's home now. The music collection included tapes of performances by Kishori Amonkar, Jeetendra Abhisheki and Mehdi Hassan. The walls were adorned with paintings by top artists. Pitambar had learnt the art of impressing the 'intellectual class' by playing Jeetendra Abhisheki's music while serving expensive alcohol. Pitambar was also hobnobbing with cynics who believed in showcasing their 'social commitment' and whose only purpose in life, despite enjoying all sorts of luxuries, was to trash the rich and their wealth. Pitambar would talk of the problems faced by farmers while enjoying a drink with such characters. He soon realised that these people found listening to Abhisheki a waste of their time. He found that by hobnobbing with both kinds of people, he gained political mileage. Politicians always needed someone who knew people outside the political arena intimately. There were many satellites that roamed around ace politicians. And Pitambar knew that the only way to remain relevant was to make himself more and more capable. Every human being has two legs and a brain. People run on their legs, but it is the brain that controls them. But some like Pitambar weren't born with two full legs. Pitambar had suffered the pain of being handicapped. And the cruel nickname 'Langdya' had continually rubbed salt in the wound. Pitambar had often wondered how he would run a race in a world where everyone else ran on two legs. But, with sheer intelligence, he ran on one and three quarters of a leg. And while he should have otherwise failed, he managed to chart unlikely routes and won. Soon the name 'Langdya' was dropped and 'Pitambar' suffixed with the honorific 'ji' adopted.

He understood early on that once he acquired a car and money in his pocket, men, otherwise superior and towering, would kowtow to him. He had seen and experienced Dhamale-sir's power, the awe which journalist Dhage inspired as well as the MLA's prestige. But their power and influence came with the posts they held. Pitambar had taken a leap beyond their horizons. He had money, fame, the company of the rich and famous, everything, without the shackles of responsibility. People like Chougule and Bhosale would come and go, but everyone pacing the corridors of power would need a 'Pitambar'. Prachi and her channel may or may not remain, but there would always be those phone calls and deals struck at midnight. But while Pitambar mused over all this, he wondered where the four-legged creature who had complimented him and made up for his handicap was. He began to miss Latthya's chatting with him while enjoying the cornflakes softened in warm milk, or while nibbling on the biscuit dipped in it. He had been witness to all of his actions. Pitambar was lost in thought, driving absentmindedly, when a cat crossed the road. Pitambar pressed down hard on the brakes. The cat crossed the road, staring at Pitambar. He peeped out of the window and shouted,

'You were saved by a whisker. Be careful when you cross.'

Without bothering to reply, the cat jumped over a wall and disappeared. Did she understand what he said? The question kept haunting Pitambar.

Chapter 10

Six months had passed. Pitambar continued his job as a deal-maker, fixer and informant. With Latthya's help he had been able to achieve seemingly impossible tasks. But with Latthya gone, that wasn't possible now. Still, Pitambar's life continued smoothly. His sharp brain helped him sail through all sorts of situations.

One morning Pitambar lay on his bed, lazing. He had spent last night drinking and was hungover. He suddenly heard a faint sound and got up with a start. It was Latthya's habit to scratch the door with his claws. He jumped up and opened the door. It was Latthya. Seeing him, Pitambar slumped to the floor.

'Look at your state, Latthya!'

Weak and emaciated, Latthya had become a shadow of his former self. His eyes didn't have the earlier spark. His fur was mud-stained, while his forehead had a gash.

Latthya let out a whimper and said, 'What can I tell you, my friend? I was burning in hell for the past six months. I couldn't get over Ghaari's death. Couldn't take the image of her body pierced by the iron rod out of my mind. I loved her to death. I had promised myself that I would never fall in love or have sex with anyone else. With her death, my lust had vanished.

'But when you hung a camera around my neck and asked me to witness the CM having sex ... I tried my best to keep my eyes shut, but I couldn't do it. I tried to calm my mind that night when I returned. But then I saw Prachi seduce you. Quite naturally, you were a willing participant and you slept soundly after that.

'It was like jumping into a pool of water to cool oneself, only to find that the water was boiling hot. It was too much for me. When Prachi left the next morning, I too left the house. I was desperately looking for a cat. The moment I found one, I jumped on her. I didn't care what she felt. It was rape. I broke the unwritten code of conduct for cats. A tomcat never has sex without explicit permission and without having made arrangements for the delivery of the cat's kittens in a safe place. Not only did I violate the code, but I also broke the promise made to Ghaari. My mind was in turmoil. As a result of the despicable act committed by me, the cats in this area decided to throw me out of their community. I roamed the streets like a lunatic ...'

Latthya was blabbering in great distress, but Pitambar couldn't understand a word of what he said. The chapter of this human-cat interaction, which had begun with Ghaari's attack on Pitambar, had ended with Latthya breaking his vow of celibacy. Pitambar was a human and cats understood their body language. But humans couldn't understand cat language. It had always been a one-way communication. Was it divine intervention then that Latthya had helped Pitambar achieve great heights? As Latthya lapped up milk from the tumbler kept on the floor, he felt like a stranger. Pitambar too suddenly felt lonesome.

❧

The next morning, Latthya left before Pitambar woke up. Pitambar had no way of finding out where he went. For six months, Pitambar kept telling himself that Latthya had left for a reason and that once his objective was fulfilled, he would return. Pitambar missed him every single moment, but the belief that he would surely return made him continue with his work. Whenever Pitambar saw a tomcat, be it in his neighbourhood or the Mantralaya, he would imagine it to be Latthya. He would at times stop and stare at a tomcat or try to engage one in a conversation. Like a battery which slowly loses its charge, the inexplicable confidence that Pitambar had had thanks to Latthya slowly waned. He desperately wanted to charge himself again by conversing with Latthya. His sharp brain was getting duller by the day. His mind had gotten used to the reinforcement that Latthya provided. He realised that not only he but his brain too was handicapped without Latthya. He recalled the conversation they had had in a taxi when he first visited Mumbai with Latthya.

'Gengane cared for Ghaari, which is why she developed some human traits; but that turned out to be the reason for her death. She would have survived had she stuck to the code of cats,' Latthya had said.

When Pitambar had asked, why are you then risking your life to help me, Latthya replied, 'That is my fate.'

Pitambar started to feel that his limp had become more pronounced since people, instead of saying 'only Pitambar can do this job', began to mutter under their breaths, 'even Pitambar couldn't do this'. He had, somewhere along the line, started believing that he was no longer handicapped and limping, thanks to the wealth and reputation he had earned. The fact was that he had always been handicapped, but the way people looked at him made him feel that they did not consider him so. But now, slowly but surely, he started seeing it in people's eyes. And after meeting Latthya, and realising that he could not converse with him any longer, a shooting pain, originating from a morbid fear of the present and future, tore through his handicapped leg. He felt as if he was enveloped by the silent, inky darkness that prevailed around the mud fort in his village.

The door bell rang very early the next morning, at around five or six a.m. Pitambar reluctantly woke up to find Gengane-master and his wife at the door. He ushered them in.

Pitambar arranged for a large breakfast while the couple went to wash up.

After his bath, Gengane-master took Pitambar aside and whispered, 'I have come here to get her checked for breast cancer.'

On hearing that, the image of the tulsi plant in Gengane-master's house catching fire suddenly flashed before Pitambar's eyes. In the ensuing smoke and light, he could see the dark shadow of Ghaari, which slowly became so huge that it covered the entire sky.

'Luckily, it's in the initial stages. The village doctor assured me that the disease can be controlled. So we have come here for further consultation,' Gengane said.

Pitambar merely nodded. He didn't even know why he was doing that. He couldn't find Latthya anywhere. He had gone away, forever, Pitambar knew that. Gengane-master's arrival once again made Pitambar aware that he was nothing but a zero; that he was back to square one. He might be wealthier than before, but other than that, he was nothing but his old self.

He quietly turned to Gengane-master, who, steeped in sorrow over his wife's illness, was addressing him repeatedly as Pitambar-ji, and said, 'Master, please! Just call me Langdya!'

www.ingramcontent.com/pod-product-compliance
Lightning Source LLC
Chambersburg PA
CBHW071300140726
47996CB00007B/2918